"With any luck, we won't have to do this again," he said

He trailed his fingertips lightly down her arms. Her skin was soft and smooth. He didn't think he'd ever touched such soft skin as hers. He lowered his mouth onto hers. Her mouth was warm and soft, her breath sweet. She responded to his kiss immediately.

"Good. Now look like you're enjoying yourself. This is looking more like sexual harassment than love."

"It's...not...love," she breathed.

"No kidding," he said against her skin. "But if you could possibly act like a warm-blooded woman, you might not ruin everything we're trying to achieve."

"Maybe you just don't warm my blood," she said haughtily, but her voice quivered at the end.

"Sweetheart, I haven't even turned the burner on and you're boiling."

Dear Reader,

As the days get shorter and the approaching holidays bring a buzz to the crisp air, nothing quite equals the joy of reuniting with family and catching up on the year's events. This month's selections all deal with family matters, be it making one's own family, dealing with family members or doing one's family duty.

Desperate to save his family ranch, the hero in Elizabeth Harbison's *Taming of the Two* (#1790) enters into a bargain that could turn a pretend relationship into the real deal. This is the second title in the SHAKESPEARE IN LOVE trilogy. A die-hard bachelor gets a taste of what being a family man is like when he rescues a beautiful stranger and her adorable infant from a deadly blizzard, in Susan Meier's *Snowbound Baby* (#1791)—part of the author's BRYANT BABY BONANZA continuity. Carol Grace continues her FAIRY TALE BRIDES miniseries with *His Sleeping Beauty* (#1792) in which a woman sheltered by her overprotective parents gains the confidence to strike out on her own after her handsome—but cynical—neighbor catches her sleepwalking in his garden! Finally, in *The Marine and Me* (#1793), the next installment in Cathie Linz's MEN OF HONOR series, a soldier determined to outwit his matchmaking grandmother and avoid the marriage landmine gets bushwhacked by his supposedly dowdy neighbor.

Be sure to come back next month when Karen Rose Smith and Shirley Jump put their own spins on Shakespeare and the Dating Game, respectively!

Happy reading.

Ann Leslie Tuttle
Associate Senior Editor

Please address questions and book requests to:
Silhouette Reader Service
U.S.: 3010 Walden Ave., P.O. Box 1325, Buffalo, NY 14269
Canadian: P.O. Box 609, Fort Erie, Ont. L2A 5X3

ELIZABETH HARBISON

Taming of the Two

Shakespeare
in Love

SILHOUETTE *Romance*

Published by Silhouette Books

America's Publisher of Contemporary Romance

Special thanks and acknowledgment are given to Elizabeth Harbison for her contribution to the SHAKESPEARE IN LOVE series.

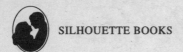

SILHOUETTE BOOKS

ISBN 0-373-19790-X

TAMING OF THE TWO

Visit Silhouette Books at www.eHarlequin.com

Printed in U.S.A.

Books by Elizabeth Harbison

Silhouette Romance

A Groom for Maggie #1239
Wife Without a Past #1258
Two Brothers and a Bride #1286
True Love Ranch #1323
Emma and the Earl #1410
Plain Jane Marries the Boss #1416
Annie and the Prince #1423
His Secret Heir #1528
A Pregnant Proposal #1553
Princess Takes a Holiday #1643
The Secret Princess #1713
Taming of the Two #1790

*Cinderella Brides

Silhouette Special Edition

Drive Me Wild #1476
Midnight Cravings #1539
How To Get Your Man #1685

Silhouette Books

Lone Star Country Club
Mission Creek Mother-To-Be

ELIZABETH HARBISON

has been an avid reader for as long as she can remember. After devouring the Nancy Drew and Trixie Belden series in grade school, she moved on to the suspense of Mary Stewart, Dorothy Eden and Daphne du Maurier, just to name a few. From there it was a natural progression to writing, although early efforts have been securely hidden away in the back of a closet.

After authoring three cookbooks, Elizabeth turned her hand to writing romances and hasn't looked back. Her second book for Silhouette Romance, *Wife Without a Past,* was a 1998 finalist for the Romance Writers of America's prestigious RITA® Award in the Best Traditional Romance category.

Elizabeth lives in Maryland with her husband, John, daughter Mary Paige, and son Jack, as well as two dogs, Bailey and Zuzu. She loves to hear from readers and you can write to her at c/o Box 1636, Germantown, MD 20875.

To Miss Erin Sears, a heroine-in-training
and Trey Sears, my boy's best pal

Chapter One

Kate Gregory couldn't believe what her sister was asking her to do. "No way," she said firmly, rolling on her squeaky wooden desk chair back to her desk, effectively turning her back on her sister. "I am not getting involved in this ridiculous plan of yours."

"But, Katie." Bianca whined behind her, like the little sister she was twenty years ago instead of the grown woman she was today. "It's a good cause. Think about it—it's *romantic*. Don't you have at least a little *tiny* bit of romance in your soul?"

Kate turned her chair around to face her sister. Now *this* was a question she could answer easily. "No. Not even a little tiny bit." No way. Romance was a gamble, and she was fed up with gambling in life.

"Kate!" Bianca was aghast. "You don't mean that."

"Oh, yes, I do." Kate smiled and turned back to the ledgers she was trying to balance for Gregory Farms, her family's Texas business, arguably the finest racehorse breeders in the west.

It was the perfect metaphor for Bianca's question, actually. For the past forty years, the Gregory family had lived through feast or famine, depending on horses' bloodlines, track conditions, weather, jockeys' health and drinking habits, voodoo and a host of other variables that couldn't be controlled.

She was looking forward to leaving. Already she'd saved a considerable amount of money, and once she hit her goal, she was moving to Dallas—close enough to be here for her father and sister if they needed her, but far enough to be out of the business—to start a new career. Probably as an elementary school teacher. Early childhood education, people in Avon Lake might be surprised to know, was what she'd gotten her college bachelor's degree in.

Some people might have said the racing life was an exciting life, but not Kate. Though she loved the animals, she could still remember some difficult early years when her family had subsisted on rice and beans and lived under constant threat of losing their home. Mother crying, father impatient, children ignored…it had been a very stressful life.

Bianca had been young then, and was lucky enough to have forgotten the worst of it. Bianca believed she had lived a life of nothing but happy prosperity.

Frankly it made her act like a bit of a spoiled brat sometimes.

Like now.

"Kat*ie*." Bianca whirled Kate's office chair around to face her. *"Please."*

"No."

"Do it for *me*."

Kate shook her head, unable to fully comprehend her sister's selfishness. "No, Bianca. I am *not* getting married for you." It was incredible that she actually had to say it at all, much less over and over again.

"You don't have to *really* get married," Bianca hastened to correct her. "Just tell Daddy you are. As long as he believes *you're* getting married, I can go ahead and plan *my* wedding."

Kate dropped her hands in her lap and looked at her sister coolly. "Tell Daddy I'm getting married."

Bianca nodded eagerly. "That's right."

"Invent a fiancé, plan a fake wedding, move into an imaginary home, and churn out and raise pretend children, presumably for the next thirty or forty years, until I retire with my nonexistent husband to bounce grandchildren I never had on my knee."

"Well…" It looked as though the light was finally dawning on Bianca. "I guess you're right."

Kate threw her hands in the air. "Hallelujah. She has *finally* seen the light."

Bianca nodded. And for a moment it seemed she had really seen the idiocy of her plan. But then she said, "We'll have to find a real guy." She tapped her chin thoughtfully.

"What?"

"Or maybe hire an actor."

Kate's jaw dropped. She gave Bianca a full ten, fifteen seconds to laugh and say she was kidding, but Bianca's face remained completely serious. "Do you hear what you're saying?" Kate asked at last. "Now you want to *hire* an *actor?* And have me pretend to *marry* him?"

"Well…"

"All this so you can mollify Dad's old-fashioned, narrow-minded, Old World chauvinism? No *way.*"

Henry Gregory was adamant that his younger daughter couldn't marry until his oldest had. But she knew it had come from the same place so many of his ideas about men and women came from: the old country and his own strict upbringing.

Before Kate's mother had died, her father had left the business of the children to her. He'd been the parent who played with the girls, the soft touch who'd always had a smile and a wink for them even when they were in trouble.

But once Kate's mother, Helen, had passed away, Henry had been like a lost animal, pacing the floors and trying to figure out the ways of the girls who, up to then, had just been playthings. Once he had the sole responsibility of raising Kate and Bianca, he had taken the job very seriously, even at the expense of losing his softer side with them.

"What else can I do?"

"You and Victor should just get married. Just *do* it. Elope. Dad will get over it."

"What if he doesn't? What if I do that and he disowns me and fires Victor?" Victor Blume was Bianca's fiancé and her father's top trainer.

"There's no way he's going to fire Victor," Kate said, "he's too valuable. And as for disowning you, that's just silly."

"How can you be so sure?"

"Because he *loves* you, Bianca, and he wants you to be happy. Even if it means going against his crazy outdated sixteenth-century notions of propriety."

"What if you're wrong?"

"I'm not." Kate looked at her sister and shook her head firmly. "Look, I *promise* he's just being an old blowhard."

Bianca looked unconvinced. "Well, if you think about it, he's really only looking after you. He doesn't want you to be a lonely old spinster. You could give him real peace of mind if you convinced him you were happily engaged to someone."

Kate gave her sister a long hard look before turning back to the desk and picking up a pen. It wasn't worth responding to such an idiotic contention. "This conversation is finished, Bianca. Close the door on your way out, would you?" She looked back at the ledger and found the thing she was looking for. An item marked "Fire Essence" with a deposit amount of four hundred and twenty-five thousand dollars.

As their supply of frozen semen from the great racehorse Fireflight dwindled, the price was going up. This was a great opportunity to convince her father to invest in something solid so he'd have a nice nest egg no matter what happened with the races.

She was going to talk to him about it right away, before he got the idea to reinvest the money into something risky. He thrived on risk—it was a real worry for her.

She picked up the phone and dialed her father's extension, but was stopped when Bianca stepped forward and took the receiver from Kate, pushing the off button.

"What about this…" Bianca began, using her persuasive voice again. "How about if you just give *dating* a try. Go out with a couple of guys, see where it leads. Maybe this whole problem would solve itself, naturally and honestly."

Kate laughed. "How altruistic of you."

"Believe it or not, Katie, I *do* care about you. It would probably do you some good to date a little bit instead of just working all the time."

Kate scoffed. "I've dated every eligible guy in town—all four of them—and, with all due respect, thanks but no thanks."

"Not *every* guy," Bianca persisted. "For example, Ben Devere's back. You never went out with *him*, even though," her voice became conspiratorial, "honestly, I think he's always had a thing for you."

Kate bristled at the mention of Ben Devere. Talk about a risk she wasn't willing to take! She'd bet on that one before and lost.

The black sheep son of the otherwise decent family who owned the property adjoining Gregory Farms, Ben Devere had always been a wild child and more than a little dangerous. When they were children, he used to set off fireworks down on the property border and when Kate cried and begged him to stop, he'd just laughed and lit another one.

When they were in high school he used to take his Jeep four-wheeling all over the pastures, which annoyed both her father and his own to no end, but which amused him enough to keep doing it. He was a wild kid, in stark contrast to her own serious nature, and they had butted heads over their differences repeatedly while growing up. In junior high school, he'd called her "Serious Sally" and she'd privately been a little afraid of his untamed ways.

But Kate could also remember, with crystal clarity, a time when she'd seen him shoot his own dog as it ran in the paddock. She'd watched the whole thing in sheer horror, then run away without looking back, vowing to never go within sixty yards of the Devere Ranch again. It was proof of what she'd already begun to suspect: Ben wasn't what he seemed at all. Sure, people *thought* he was charming and smart, and more than one girl—heaven knew!—had fallen for his charisma. But the fact was, Ben Devere wasn't who he appeared to be.

That conclusion made Kate more comfortable with what he'd done to her.

Ben had been regarded in high school and in town as a hot playboy; the kind of guy girls wouldn't count on to call them in the morning, but with whom they were willing to take the chance nonetheless. If the stories were true, scores of women had fallen prey to his charms. Even Kate had kissed him once at a party, the summer after their senior year. It had been a hell of a kiss, and for a few weeks afterward, she'd harbored hopes that he would call and that perhaps…well, whatever. Later, she realized it had only been a heat of the moment hormonal rush for Ben.

But *perhaps* had never come and Kate had learned to regret having admitted to her affection for him. She'd also learned to regret having trusted him. If his friend Lou Parker was to be believed, he'd only been with Kate as a joke, the response to a dare. Lou's subsequent advances on her had only served to make the insult that much greater.

Shortly after that, Ben Devere had left town and, after the humiliation she'd been through, she was glad to see the back of him. She'd hoped he'd never come back.

But now he had.

And her sister, who should have known better, was actually suggesting she *date* him.

"No way," she said to Bianca, and reached down to pet her dog, Sierra, who was lying at her feet. She'd had the retriever for twelve years now, and he was getting old and thin, but he was a member of the family. "I'd rather become a nun. Now let me get back to work, I have to talk to Dad about the finances."

Bianca perched her hands on her slender hips. "So that's it? We're just not talking about my *marriage* anymore?"

"No, I'd be glad to talk about your marriage. It's *my* marriage, or the lack thereof, that I'm not talking about anymore."

"Fine." Bianca smirked. "Then I don't have anything else to say to you at all." She huffed out of the room and Kate watched her go with mild irritation.

It had always been this way with Bianca. She should have been used to it by now, but somehow she always hoped her sister would rise to the occasion and take the high road.

Oh, well. She didn't have the time or the emotional cash to spend worrying about it now. She had to balance these books, and while a half million dollars was a nice thing to add to any accounting ledger, she was uncomfortable with keeping it in the regular accounts.

She picked up the phone again to call her father.

Ben Devere drove the muddy side roads from his farm to Gregory Farms slowly, trying to talk himself out of his mission even while he accelerated toward it.

He couldn't believe he had to ask Kate Gregory—of all people!—for a favor, especially one that amounted to his only hope of saving his late father's farm for his mother. Kate Gregory hated him.

Growing up, he'd had a little bit of a crush on Kate. Well, maybe *crush* was too strong a word. But he'd always noticed her. While the rest of the world had fawned over her younger sister's blond-haired-and-blue-eyed version of Kewpie doll beauty, Ben had been fascinated by Kate's more subtle—but infinitely more interesting—assets.

The long chestnut hair didn't look like gold, the way they said Bianca's did, but it glowed like amber in the sunlight, with hundreds of different variations of brown and auburn painting the strands. Ben could have studied it for hours without getting bored.

And her eyes—they were vivid green and just shy of catlike. They were warm and cool at the same time. Intelligent and alluring, and never lined with the unnatural colors so many of the girls wore.

Ben often thought Kate said a lot more with her eyes than she did with her voice.

Then there was her body. He took a breath just thinking about it. Tight and strong and slender. Ben guessed that while Bianca sat on her cushiony behind and asked the ranch hands to bring her bonbons, Kate did the heavy work around the place.

Privately, Ben suspected it was Kate who had kept Gregory Farms such formidable competition for the Devere Ranch for so many years, which made her an enemy in a sense, but an admirable one. All of which made it doubly hard to have to ask her for her help now, since it was to keep the competition in business.

Ben reminded himself how important this was for his mother's quality of life.

The last time he'd seen Kate had been one of the worst days of his life. His old dog, Banjo, who had seen him through the loneliest of his childhood years straight through college, had stayed out one night and gotten into a tangle with a rabid raccoon. It hadn't taken long to figure out what was wrong, and when the vet had advised them to take Banjo out back, Ben wouldn't let anyone go except for himself. It was a private thing, between him and his old pal.

Pulling that trigger had been the worst moment of his life, and it had felt as though it had taken a year.

No sooner was it over with, and the dog had hit the ground, had Ben heard a gasp and turned to see Kate Gregory running across the lower pasture toward her house. She must have known what was going on; the word had gotten out as a warning to all the local residents of what had happened.

Yet, when she'd seen Ben have to shoot his own dog, she hadn't even mustered a single word of sympathy. She'd just run off into the sunset, literally *and* figuratively.

That's the way Kate had always been—aloof, detached. Like no one could really get close to her or touch her heart.

He pulled his Jeep to a halt outside the main barn and got out. He took a deep breath. He didn't want to do it. He just had to remind himself that, if he was careful, he might just score the one thing that could save his family's farm. His feet crunched the gravel below him as he took slow steps toward the barn office.

"Ben?"

He turned.

The surprised voice belonged to none other than the platinum-haired Bianca, who was coming from the direction of the office. "Is that Ben Devere?"

"That's right."

"Good Lord, we were just talking about you."

"We? We who?" This was weird. He didn't even know anyone knew he was back. "And what were you saying?"

"Oh." She hesitated just long enough to imply she was hiding something. "Nothing, really. Just that you were here in town. So what brings you here?"

This was it. Time to take that step. "I was hoping to see Kate."

"Oh, were you?" Bianca raised an eyebrow. "How interesting! Now, why is that? You're not planning to ask my single sister out on a date of some sort, are you?"

"Um, no." He frowned. That was a strange question. "It was a business matter."

Bianca's face fell and her lips puffed into that famous Bianca Gregory pout. "Oh. Darn."

He felt a little like he'd stepped into someone else's bizarre dream. "I'm sorry…what?"

Bianca shrugged with the drama of a four-year-old child. "Nothing. Never mind."

Ben looked down at the earth beneath his feet and briefly weighed the relative merits of selling the farm and moving his mother to a smaller place, closer to him, versus begging the Gregory girls for their help.

Saving the farm won, of course. "Look, I understand you have the capability of siring a mare by Fireflight." It was awkward but he couldn't think of another way to word it. Word underground was that the Gregorys had somehow acquired frozen genetic material from one of the finest racehorses ever to hit the turf and if there was one thing that could save his farm, it was a foal or two by Fireflight.

Dawning understanding came into Bianca's pale blue eyes. "Oo-oh, I see. You're here to make a purchase."

"Depending on the cost, yes." That was where this conversation was going to get really sticky. His finances were limited and he could only bluff so far before they, potentially, made him look like the desperate man he was. "So what's your price?"

Bianca looked at him, raising her finger to her mouth and looking him over as she considered. "From what I hear, the Devere Ranch doesn't have a whole lot of money, Ben."

"Don't listen to everything you hear."

"Fireflight's worth a whole lot."

"Potentially." He tried to look casual. "You never know what you're gonna end up with. Artificial insemination of a mare…well, it's a hell of a gamble. You know that."

She gave a nonconcessionary nod. "It's a gamble a lot of people are willing to pay a hell of a lot of money for." She eyed him. "Victor's working a colt out at the track every morning, and he says the times are absolutely amazing. He may even beat his sire. So I'm thinking it's a pretty safe bet anyone who sires a mare by Fireflight will end up with a profit in the end. That is, if they can pay up front."

"What are we talking about?"

"Half a million."

He couldn't shell out more than a quarter million. Not for such a risky chance as this. After all, the money was going to be coming out of *his* pocket, not the ranch's. "Well, Bianca, this business being what it is, I think I'd rather just take a chance with what I've got." He gave a short nod and started back toward his truck.

"I think I might know a way you can take it for free, though," Bianca called behind him in a singsong voice.

This was no time to stand on pride. He stopped and turned back to her, cautiously keeping his face impassive. "Who do I have to kill?"

She laughed. "You only have to date my sister."

She hadn't said what he thought she'd said. Surely she wasn't suggesting it was worth five hundred grand to Kate to have a date. "What are you talking about?"

Bianca gave a slow smile and sauntered over toward him. "I need a little favor. If you succeed, you get Fireflight *and* my sister, and you have a chance at real happiness. If you don't succeed—" she shrugged "—well, you're no worse off than you are now. What do you say, are you a betting man, Ben Devere?"

Chapter Two

It was a chilly, misty morning and Kate could hear the thundering hoofbeats on the turf long before the horse actually appeared from the mist, running all-out, white puffs of steam coming from his nose.

He was beautiful.

Her father had named the horse Kate's Flight, in honor of her and in reference to his sire, so she felt a special affinity for the chestnut stallion. As much as she hated the gamble of this lifestyle, she loved the majesty of the animals and the heart they showed every time they hit the track.

The story of Black Gold—crossing the finish line with a shattered leg, to complete his final win—was never completely out of her mind. The horses loved to run and, more than that, they loved to *win,* there was no doubt about it.

So she smiled as she watched Kate's Flight barrel past in the predawn light.

"Quite a horse," a voice behind her said.

She turned to see a man walking toward her through the mist. He was tall and dark-haired, with piercing dark eyes and the sort of chiseled jawline usually reserved for the cover of a romance novel. He looked familiar, but it took her a moment to realize why.

When she did, it was with a start. "So it's not a rumor. The prodigal son has returned."

He smiled, that movie star smile she remembered better than she ought to. "I'm as surprised as anyone."

She'd heard rumors that the Devere Ranch was in trouble. "Here on family business?"

He nodded.

She looked at him for a moment, then said, "Look, I'm sorry things aren't going well over there. I was sorry to hear about your dad's death last year. Your mom must really miss him a lot."

He shrugged, noncommittal.

"I really hope you can help her get it all straightened out," Kate offered.

He looked at her with surprise in his eyes. "I appreciate that."

"So what brings you here this morning? I haven't seen any of your trainers around."

"Actually, I'm here to see *your* trainer." He nodded toward Victor and Kate's Flight. "Or, more specifically, your horse."

"Really? Why's that?"

He kept his eyes fastened on the horse's workout. "I've got a colt I think I can run against him. I just wanted to check him out first and talk to Victor about it."

"Oh." She thought about that for a moment. It made sense. If he could run a colt against the son of Fireflight and win, it would do wonders for the credibility of Devere's breeding. "I see."

"Does that worry you?"

Everything that had anything to do with failing on the track and losing financial security worried her. "Not at all."

He nodded, his tightened jaw betraying an attempt not to smile. "Good."

"I mean it."

"I'm sure you do."

She frowned and turned back to the track, where Victor was walking toward them. He was small but powerfully built. Every time Kate saw him, the thought came to her that he was shaped like a shoe horn.

"Hey, Kate." He waved a meaty arm at her. "You take that dog to the vet yet?"

Victor had been telling her Sierra was getting too thin, so, even though she thought it was old age, she'd finally given in and made an appointment. "We're going this afternoon."

"Good girl. Better to check it out."

"I agree."

He nodded and turned to Ben. "Hey, Ben." He smiled and put a hand out. "Good to see you again."

Ben shook his hand. "Thanks. Looks like you've got a winner on your hands out there."

"You know it."

"How would you feel about running him up against one of mine?"

Victor laughed and ran a hand through his sandy-blond hair. "Bring it on." He looked behind him and signaled to the jockey on Kate's Flight. "You talking about that colt from Sunuawa?"

Ben smiled and nodded. "You've heard."

"Hey, word travels. But I'd love to see what your boy can do. You know where to find us." He turned to Kate and said, "I don't want to interrupt you two, so I'll see you later."

"You're not interrupting *us!*" she said quickly, but he was already leaving. Obviously, Bianca had shared her harebrained plan about Kate and Ben with him.

She watched him go, wondering what on earth to say to Ben, who was still standing beside her.

"So I hear you've got the technology for Fireflight to sire more," Ben said, looking sideways at her.

"It's not for sale," she said quickly.

"No?" He looked surprised. "I was misinformed, then."

"It *was* for sale. My father sold some, but there's very little left now. As I'm sure you can imagine, offering Fireflight's bloodlines is our ace in the hole." She thought about that for a moment. "So to speak."

"Hmm." He nodded, keeping his eyes on the track and the horses that were running against each other. Kate's Flight was leading the competition by a considerable margin. "Not at any price, huh?"

"Nope." Then, as an afterthought, she added, "Sorry."

"No problem." His words were casual, but when Kate glanced at him she thought he looked grave.

"Hey!" a voice barked behind them.

Kate turned to face a squat, wizened old woman she'd noticed several times running the betting windows.

"One of you Katherine Gregory?"

Kate had to work to keep from laughing. "That would be me," she said, adding the obvious, "Not him."

The woman didn't so much as crack a smile. "There's a phone call for you up in the shop."

Kate frowned. "That's weird. Did they say who it was?"

"Think it's your father or something." The woman gave an exaggeratedly disinterested shrug. "He said he couldn't get through on your cell phone."

"That's crazy. I don't need to go all the way to the track shop to get a call." She patted her pocket, looking for the phone she was sure had been there earlier. But it was gone. "Hmm. Okay, I guess I *do* need to go all the way up to the shop." She started toward the main building, tossing over her shoulder, "Nice talking to you, Ben."

He raised a hand in response.

The woman asked, "Ben Devere?"

"That's right," he said slowly.

"There's a telephone message for you there, as well."

Kate paused. "We *both* got phone calls up there?"

"Guess so," the woman said.

Ben looked at Kate with a frown. "You don't suppose that fence is down between the properties again, do you?"

She groaned. "I hope not. That was a mess."

"We'd better go see what's going on."

They hurried to the building, up the stairs and into the darkened shop. "You'd think she could have left the lights on, at least," Kate commented, feeling her way to the counter, where she remembered having seen a phone before.

"There's something strange about this," Ben said.

The door closed behind them and they both looked back at it for a moment. Then Ben found the light switch and the room was flooded with fluorescent glow.

Kate found the phone and picked it up, looking to see which line was on hold.

None of them were.

"For Pete's sake." She pressed line one and dialed her father's number.

As soon as he answered, she asked, "Is everything okay?"

"Everything's fine, Katherine," he said. "Why?"

She frowned. "They said you were trying to get hold of me and couldn't get through on my cell phone."

"That's nonsense," her father said to her. "I didn't try to call you."

She was somewhat relieved, even while she was flummoxed. "What about Bianca? Where is she?"

"She's at the track with Victor. With you, too, I guess, if you're there."

She watched as Ben poked around, looking for the message that had supposedly been left for him. An uneasy feeling snaked into Kate's stomach.

"I gotta go, Dad. I'll talk to you later." She hung up the phone and rushed to the door.

"Hey, what's going on?" Ben asked. "What's the emergency?"

She got to the door and tried it.

It was locked.

Exactly as she'd suspected.

"I don't think there is an emergency," she said, not adding that there was *going* to be one just as soon as she got out of here and wrapped her hands around Bianca's neck. "There's been some sort of…mistake." She jiggled the doorknob, hoping to throw the lock.

"Is that *locked?*"

Kate turned around and leaned her back against the cool door. "Yes, it is."

"So we're locked in here?"

"Yes, we are."

He heaved a sigh and went over to the phone, muttering something about idiots in charge. He lifted the receiver and pushed a button. Then another. And another.

Then he tapped on the receiver button.

Kate watched with growing trepidation. "What's wrong?"

"Phone's dead."

"I just used it."

"Well, now it's dead."

"Do you have a cell phone?"

"No."

This pushed her panic buttons. "What do you mean, no? How can you not have a cell phone?"

"I notice you don't, either."

"Yes, but I *did.*"

He looked at her too patiently. "Then where is it?"

"It must have fallen out of my pocket. Or something." At this point she was sure Bianca was behind this somehow.

"Whatever. Let's stop talking about what we *can't* do and figure out what we *can.*" He frowned and looked around. "First thing is, we should look for keys."

"Okay. Good." Hope surged in Kate. Surely, Bianca hadn't been that thorough. They began riffling under the counter and in the cash register, looking for a key.

At one point they both put their hands in the same

cubbyhole at the same time and Kate pulled her hand back as though she'd touched a snake.

Ben looked at her for a moment. "Something wrong?"

"No, I—" What could she say? How could she explain what looked like such a distasteful reflex? "I was startled."

He kept feeling around the cubby before pronouncing, "And for nothing. There's nothing here." He stepped back and folded his arms in front of him. "We'll have to figure something else out."

"We could break the window," Kate suggested, gesturing toward what she thought was obviously the only thing left they could do.

"Kate, it's a racetrack. They plan for security breaches. That's not glass. It's thick Lucite. You couldn't break it if you tried. Not without a power tool."

"Do they sell power tools in here?" she asked halfheartedly.

"Afraid not."

They both looked at the inventory of horse-themed T-shirts and sweatshirts, key chains and the like.

"If it wouldn't appeal to a thirteen-year-old girl, I don't think they sell it here," Ben concluded.

Panic began to rise in Kate's chest. "So, wait a

minute, you're saying that we actually *can't* get out of here? We're *stuck?*"

He looked as if he was ready to give some smart-aleck answer until he looked into Kate's eyes. Then his expression softened and he said, "I didn't say that. We haven't exhausted all the possibilities yet. Not by a long shot." But he looked doubtful.

She didn't care, she'd take it. "I have a Swiss army knife, do you think we can do something with that?"

"Hand it over. Let's see."

She reached into her pocket, thinking what a good thing it was that she'd gotten a splinter earlier because she'd ended up pocketing the knife after using the tweezers in it.

But when she handed it to him, he looked at it dubiously.

"What's wrong?" she asked.

"Well." He turned the knife over in his hand and opened the small blade. "I was sort of picturing something a little bigger. But this might do."

He went to the door and started working at the lock.

Kate went up behind him and watched over his shoulder. "Guess those years of juvenile delinquency might just be coming in handy, huh?"

He shot a look at her. "I'd hardly say I was a juvenile delinquent." He worked more on the knob and said, without looking back, "But yeah, I guess you could say so."

There was a click and for a moment they both sucked in their breath in anticipation. But when he tried the knob, it was still unmovable.

He closed the knife and started to hand it back to her.

"You can't give up," she said.

"I've got to. This place is built with security in mind. They designed it exactly so that people couldn't do what we're trying to do now."

"So that's it? You're just…quitting?"

He laughed softly. "Well, it's not like we're going to die here. They open the shop a couple of hours before post time. Someone will be here soon."

Kate looked at her watch. "It's six-thirty in the morning," she said, her breath feeling tight. "Post time isn't until seven o'clock tonight."

He looked pained. "That's right. I was thinking 1:00 p.m."

"Only on Sundays." She began to knead her hands in front of her, noticing her palms were growing damp.

He sighed and leaned back against the counter. "Well, this bites the big one, that's for sure."

To Kate, it felt as if the walls were closing in. "We've got to get out of here."

"We can't," he said absently. "God, you have always been such a bundle of nerves."

"I have not!"

He met her eyes. "Sure you have. Always."

Anger rose in her, temporarily obscuring her growing claustrophobia. "How dare you say something like that to me. You, of all people, who did everything you could to *make* me a bundle of nerves."

He shook his head. "I didn't do anything any kid my age wouldn't have done."

"You did *everything* that *no* other kid your age was doing. We all watched, amazed, as you put glue on the teachers' chairs and gum on the chalkboard and—"

"Nothing scary about that."

"Well, no, not about *that*—"

"So what're you blaming me for?"

She gave a humorless spike of a laugh. "Plenty. Believe me."

He waved the notion away with his hand. "That's bull. But it's totally consistent bull. You *always* made a bigger deal of things than you had to."

"So I was nervous and hysterical, is that what you're saying?"

He looked her up and down. "That's about the size of it."

"Meanwhile, you were perfect."

"Not perfect." He cocked his head fractionally

and very obviously tried to keep from smiling. "Just normal."

She made a sound of disgust and threw her hands into the air. "You are amazing." She walked back to the door to try to figure out some way to work it open. "Absolutely amazing."

"Thanks," he said behind her. "I've heard that, but I never thought I'd hear it from you."

She glanced back at him. "It wasn't a compliment."

This time he did smile. "I know."

She gave him the evil eye as best she could. "Please tell me you're not staying long."

He shook his head. "Just until about seven tonight."

"Wha—" She frowned. "You know I mean in town, not in this shop."

"Ah, in town. Well, now. That depends how quickly I can get the farm back into shape."

"Oh, good Lord, that could take forever," she said before she realized what she was saying. She quickly added, "You've been in the business long enough to know that every time you think you've got it figured out, fate throws you another curve ball."

He studied her for a moment before giving a single nod. "I'm not looking to hit the ball out of the park."

He didn't offer any more information and even though Kate wanted to know more about what he'd done in the ten years he'd been away, she got the distinct impression that she shouldn't ask for more.

In fact, she decided her time would probably be much better spent praying vehemently that someone would come to let them out of here, so she didn't have to spend any more time at all making awkward small talk with Ben.

But at least he'd distracted her from her feeling of claustrophobia. There was something to be said for that, because for a moment there she'd actually thought she might totally lose it.

Why, she couldn't say. She'd never been claustrophobic before. Those close to her might say she was a little high-strung at times, but never irrational.

Looking at Ben now, she almost wondered if he'd picked up on her panic and tried to help her by purposely getting her mad instead of scared.

For the briefest moment, her heart softened toward him. But then she remembered that Ben Devere didn't make selfless gestures for anyone, least of all for Kate Gregory.

Chapter Three

Three hours later they were still stuck in the shop and they had exhausted absolutely every possibility, and more than a few long shots, to free themselves.

"I saw this TV show once," Kate said, "where they held a lit match up to the smoke detectors to set off the alarm."

"I saw that one. The sprinklers went off and they got soaked."

"But they got saved."

"We're not in danger, Kate. We don't actually need to go to extraordinary lengths to get out of here before we run out of air, or die of dehydration or anything." He went to the fridge and took out a cola and held it up in offer.

Kate shook her head, so he closed the door and opened the cola for himself, before sitting back down to drink it along with the bag of cheese snacks he'd pilfered from the register stand.

"That stuff'll kill you," Kate commented, watching him eat the junk food. "That's probably more dangerous than being stuck in here."

He laughed out loud. "Doing laundry is more dangerous than being stuck in here."

She shrugged and returned her attention to the gossip magazine she'd found on the stand with the racing forms.

"What about you? Reading that garbage probably isn't good for you."

She set the magazine down and looked at him patiently. "It's better than listening to you."

"Maybe."

She returned her attention to the magazine.

"Then again, at least I tell the truth."

She set the magazine down again. "As opposed to who? Me or this magazine?"

He popped a cheese snack in his mouth and raised his eyebrows. "Guilty conscience?"

"Not at all. It just sounded as if you were accusing me of something and I was wondering what it was."

"Hmm."

"Don't *hmm* me, what were you getting at? I *never* lie!"

"Never?"

She shook her head. "Absolutely never."

"So if your sister asks if she looks fat in a certain pair of jeans—and you think she does—you tell her the truth, even if you think she does."

Jeez, that situation had come up just last week. How did he know? "My sister isn't fat."

"I didn't say she was. I only asked if you would tell her the truth if she wanted to know something like that."

Kate sighed. "I said I was honest, I didn't say I was mean."

"Which is it? Are you honest all the time or not? If you're honest all the time, then it's inevitable that sometimes you're going to have to be mean."

"I think a person can be honest *and* tactful."

He took a swig of his cola. "Most people aren't."

She wasn't sure what to say. She couldn't honestly say she'd never told a little white lie. Who could? But if she admitted that to him, he'd pounce on her.

So instead she decided to put the heat on him. "What about you? Do you lie?"

"Me?" He wasn't biting. "Sure. All the time."

She couldn't believe he was admitting it. "Are you serious?"

"Absolutely." He gave a nod. "Ask me if you look fat in those jeans."

She felt the blood rush to her face. "No, thanks," she said, then had to wonder if she could believe an admitted liar when he said he was telling the truth.

He shrugged. "Suit yourself."

"I will."

"But you don't."

"What?"

"You don't look fat. You look amazing in those jeans. I noticed it as soon as I saw you this morning."

Her face flushed again, only this time with foolish pride. Then she remembered the context of their conversation. "Oh, I see, this is one of your lies, right? You got me."

"No, that was the truth. But even if you looked like an elephant in spandex, I wouldn't say that to you."

"Thanks." She frowned. "I think."

He popped the last cheese snack into his mouth and crumpled the plastic bag. "You're welcome." He tossed the bag neatly into the trash can from a distance of about ten feet.

She watched him for a minute. "I don't get you, Ben."

He looked surprised. "What's to get?"

She looked into his warm brown eyes and tried to figure out who he was underneath it all. She couldn't even guess.

Before she could answer him, there was a key at the door and they both sprang to their feet, Ben wiping crumbs from his shirt and Kate folding the magazine neatly into its original shape.

They waited for what seemed like ages until the door finally creaked open and the familiar face of old Mr. Warner peered in.

He shrieked upon seeing Ben and Kate, then held his hand to his chest and asked, "What in tarnation are you two doing in here?"

"We got locked in," Kate explained. "I'm so sorry if we startled you."

"You didn't startle me," the old man said, but his pink cheeks told another story. "I just...that is... what in blazes were you doing here in the first place?"

"Someone told us we had phone messages up here," Ben said.

Mr. Warner looked skeptical. "Since when do the Deveres and the Gregorys get their phone calls in the track shop?"

It *did* sound foolish, Kate had to concede. "Someone told us that was the case," she said. "Of course it didn't sound right, but we came to check in case there was an emergency at home. Turns out someone was just playing some sort of prank on us so they could lock us in." She would kill Bianca. She would kill her gladly.

Mr. Warner tightened his lips into a thin line and looked from Ben to Kate and back again, before saying, "Get on out of here, you two. Before I take inventory and charge you for all the junk food you've been eating." He looked at Ben. "I'm talking to you, Mr. Devere."

Ben smiled. "Put it on my tab."

"Indeed I will."

Kate watched the exchange with something like admiration. Ben had always had the gift of being at ease with people, no matter how much older or crankier they were. He was a charmer, no doubt about it.

Fortunately she was long over falling for his brand of charm.

"You doing all right?" he asked her seriously when at last they emerged into the main building.

"I'm fine," she said, humiliated beyond words that she had made the mistake of showing her weakness to him. But that was the definition of weakness, at least of her particular brand of claustrophobia; there was no hiding it. "Thanks.

"So I guess…" Their ordeal over, she wasn't sure how to leave things. "I'll see you later."

He nodded. "By the way, Kate?"

"Hmm?"

"Seriously. You look amazing in those jeans." He winked and before she could react, he was ambling down the hall, whistling tunelessly to himself.

And she was watching him go, reluctantly appreciating the fit of his own jeans.

"That was going too far," Kate stormed at her sister when she got home. "I can't *believe* you would do that just to try and, what, get me to fall for some guy? What *was* your aim?"

Bianca turned in her vanity chair to face Kate, her blue eyes wide. "What did I do? What are you talking about?"

"Don't you play innocent with me, Bianca Gregory."

Bianca splayed her arms. "I'm not! What are you talking about?"

"I'm talking about you locking me in the track shop with Ben Devere this morning, as if you don't know."

"What?"

"I would never have done something like that to you," Kate went on. *"Never."*

"But I wouldn't, either." Bianca's big eyes filled with tears. "I wasn't even at the track this morning!"

"Really? Then why did Dad say you were? Right before the phone lines got cut off, I mean."

She had to hand it to her, Bianca did look genuinely puzzled. "I told Dad I was going to the track because I didn't want him to know where I was really going!"

"And where was that?"

Bianca opened the top drawer of her vanity, took something out and tossed it to Kate.

A package of birth control pills.

With today's date.

"I was at the doctor getting those." Bianca sniffed. "I didn't want to tell Daddy because—well, you know. Because I don't want him to know I'm—"

Kate held up her hand. "I get it. I know." She softened her voice some. "So you really weren't at the track?"

"No!"

"And you had nothing to do with locking Ben and me up?"

"I told you I wouldn't do that." She bit her lower lip. "But Victor and I *did* talk about you and Ben maybe getting together." She shrugged. "I suppose it's possible that Victor…you know…tried to help nature move along with the two of you. If he did it, I'm sure he didn't mean any harm. But his heart was in the right place. I mean, we've all known forever that you and Ben had a thing for each other."

"Why would you say that? That is absolutely untrue."

Bianca shrugged. "Whatever. Forget I mentioned it. Where are you going?"

"I have to take Sierra to the vet."

"Oh, thank goodness. He's been acting weird today."

That stopped Kate. "What do you mean?"

"He's sort of shaky, you know? Nothing obvious, he just didn't seem like himself."

Dread formed in Kate's chest. "I'm sure it's nothing."

Bianca's face was etched with concern. "Me, too."

But that didn't keep Kate from worrying all the way down to her office. When she got there, she opened the door, fully expecting to be relieved by the sight of a normal Sierra coming toward her with his tail wagging.

Instead she found her dog, her companion of more than a decade, stumbling around in circles, the whites of his eyes more visible than the brown pupils that were turned up toward the corners.

"Sierra!" She ran to him, putting her arms out to stop the crazy stumbling. The dog paused in her arms, but didn't seem to recognize her presence. Up close the crossed eyes were even more frightening. He was having a seizure of some sort, maybe a stroke.

With shaking hands, she tried to guide him to the door by the collar, but it was slow going and the dog was unable to walk in a straight line.

"Come on, boy," she said in a voice that was more alarming to him than soothing, she knew. A sob was caught in her throat and she was shaking so intensely inside that she felt as though she'd had a hundred cups of coffee. "Come on, you can do it. Let's get in the car and go to the doctor. You'll be okay."

Sierra lurched forward, then spilled onto his side.

Panic filled Kate's breast and, with strength from adrenaline, she lifted the dog and started to carry him to her car.

Chapter Four

Ben wasn't sure what got into him, but instead of driving back to his own farm, he found himself driving over to Gregory Farms.

For some reason, he felt as though he really ought to apologize to Kate. Not that it was his fault they'd gotten locked in or anything, but he could have been a little kinder about the panic she'd obviously been feeling. True, he'd tried to help by distracting her into being angry instead of scared—it had always been easy to make Kate Gregory angry—but upon further consideration, he wondered if he'd made the right choice. After all, she'd probably been in need of kindness and understanding, but what he'd given her was…well, it was far from it.

So it was only right that he should apologize.

But it was only smart, too. If he had any hope of Bianca honoring the deal she'd proposed, he had to make nice with her. So there was a double benefit to apologizing, even though it rubbed him the wrong way to do so.

He pulled his Jeep up outside the barn where the offices were located and put it into park. It took a moment or two of deep breathing to gather the gumption to get out of the car and seek Kate out. But no sooner had he gotten out and slammed the door shut, than Kate came out of the office, struggling under the weight of a large golden retriever she was trying to carry.

"Kate? What are you doing?"

"Sierra." She tried to catch her breath. "Something's wrong. I have to get him to the vet."

"Slow down." Ben hurried to her and helped her set the dog down before she dropped him.

Immediately the animal began turning in circles, his left eye screwed up in the corner and his left ear flopping lower than the right.

Ben had seen this before. The dog was suffering from a stroke.

"Whoa, boy." He scooped the dog into his arms and said, "Open the back door of my Jeep."

She jumped at his order, for once not arguing.

He carefully placed the suffering animal into the back seat and said to Kate, "I'll drive, just tell me where to go."

There was no false bravado now, just gratitude, in her eyes and in her voice. "Thank you." She climbed in next to the dog and said, "It's the Lake Avon Veterinary Clinic on Zavala Street."

Ben knew it well, and he hurried to start the car and jerked it into drive. It was difficult to strike a balance between the rush he needed to put on to get to the vet and the care he knew he needed to take with the sick dog and Kate in the back seat.

The drive there seemed interminable and Ben kept his hands firmly on the wheel, eyes straight ahead, as he listened to Kate trying to soothe the sick animal behind him.

It broke his heart.

He knew where this was headed. He'd been there before. There were few things in life more difficult than saying goodbye to a beloved pet, and Kate had had this dog for as far back as he could remember. This was going to be torture for her.

He pulled up to the emergency entrance of the veterinary office and got out before Kate could collect herself. He threw open the back door and reached in for the dog. "Easy, boy," he said.

"I'll help," Kate said, scrambling out of the vehicle.

"I've got him."

"Please." She put a hand on Ben's forearm. "I want to be there for him. He needs me. He's scared."

"You're right." Ben swallowed the lump of emotion that was forming in his throat and nodded. He carried the dog into the vet's office while Kate stayed nearby, her hand on the dog's head, stroking and saying soothing things to the sick animal.

It was on the tip of his tongue to tell her about when he'd lost his dog, but he didn't want to make this about him. It was about Kate and her dog now.

Watching her now, he realized she wasn't as cold as he'd always thought. Maybe it was just men she was cold toward.

Or maybe it was just Ben.

The ensuing scene, when they got into the office, was fast and confusing. Kate had already had an appointment, so they were prepared to see her come in with the dog, but they weren't prepared for the condition the dog was in.

Kate and the animal were rushed into an examining room and Ben hung back and watched them go, opting to wait in the waiting room to see what Kate would need him to do.

It seemed like forever that he waited, while people came and went, all of them bearing a resemblance—sometimes a striking one—to their pet. Ben watched, trying to remain objective; trying not to think about the times he'd had to bring his own pets into this very office.

Trying not to think about the time he'd had to put Banjo out of his misery alone in the lower field, rather than try to drive a rabid animal to the office by himself.

It was hard to say how much time had passed but when Kate finally emerged from the back room, the sun had gone down and it was dark outside, except for the streetlamps. The last of the patients had either been checked in or checked out, so Ben was the only one in the waiting room.

Kate came out, looking red-eyed and weary, but when she saw Ben her expression turned to one of surprise. "You're still here?"

What the hell had she thought? That he'd cut out at a time like this. "Yeah, I'm still here."

She looked as if she couldn't quite believe it. "I had no idea you'd been waiting here all this time."

"Well, I figured you'd need a ride home. You weren't planning on pitching your tent here forever, were you?"

She gave a weak laugh and shook her head. "No, thanks."

He smiled at her. "So what's going on with the dog?"

She took a long, shuddering breath. "Turns out it's just an equilibrium thing from an ear infection. It's pretty bad infection, though, so that added to his disorientation."

"Are they keeping him overnight?"

She nodded. "They're going to do an MRI and all that." She sniffed. "Funny thing was, as soon as we got into the back offices, he was just back to normal." She snapped her fingers. "Like that."

"So maybe he'll be okay. Maybe it *is* as simple as an ear infection or something."

Kate looked at him with hope in her eyes. "Do you think so? Really?"

He should have admitted that he didn't know what he was talking about, that he only hoped to make her feel better, but he couldn't take that hope out of her eyes. "Sure. Absolutely." Then, so he didn't have to elaborate on something he knew next to nothing about, he said, "Now, let's go home. There's nothing more you can do for Sierra tonight."

She looked doubtfully at the door to the back room, then back at Ben. "I guess you're right. They probably won't let me sleep in the waiting room."

He eyed the uncomfortable wooden chairs and

said, "I would be amazed if you could even get a minute or two of sleep in here. Come on. Let's go."

He ushered her out to the Jeep and into the front seat, then he walked around to his own door and paused before opening it. This had been a strange day. This morning he and Kate had been like bulls butting heads in a bullring—how had he ended up being the one person who was there for her at such an emotional time? What was wrong with her family that *they* weren't here?

He didn't wonder for long. It only took a moment to remember this was Kate Gregory he was thinking of, and she was no ordinary person when it came to emotion. If her family hadn't been there for her, there was only one explanation: she hadn't told them she needed them.

That was a lot more consistent with what he knew of the Gregorys.

He got into the car and started it up, putting it into gear a lot more slowly than he had when the sick dog was in the Jeep.

Kate leaned back against the seat and looked out the moon roof. "There's Sirius," she commented. "The dog star. Do you think that's a good omen, or a bad one?"

Ben glanced at the sky and saw the bright star. "It's got to be a good one." Then he looked at her.

"I hope so." She sighed and turned her head to look out the window. "I can't thank you enough for helping me today," she said without turning to him. "I thought I could just take him to the vet and…" She bowed her head and didn't speak for a moment. "It's just a good thing you came along. Thank you."

"Glad I could help."

She turned to him. "How *did* you end up at my place at that moment anyway?"

It was a wonder it had taken her this long to question him on it. "I was coming to see you. To apologize if I was insensitive earlier."

She gave a dry laugh. "Earlier, when I was a different kind of emotional mess. Oh, boy, you've seen me at my worst twice over today."

"If that's your worst, it's really not so bad," he said, keeping his eyes on the road.

"I'm not buying that, but it's nice of you to say."

He felt her look over at him.

He kept his gaze averted, glancing at the Texas Lights Hotel as they passed rather than meet the gaze he felt too hotly on him.

"But, seriously, why did you come back? It's not as if you have to see me in your everyday life."

"No," he agreed slowly. "But maybe for a while…" He glanced at her. "It's come to my attention that we might be able to help each other…."

* * *

Kate felt an unpleasant jolt of emotion. "Help each other how?" she asked cautiously.

Ben hesitated before confiding, "Your sister told me what she's up to."

No point in panicking. Not yet, at least. She'd done it too many times today already. "Up to how? I'm sorry, I don't know what you mean."

"Up to as far as trying to set you up with a guy," he said, flat-out. "So she and Victor can get married."

Kate was surprised. Had Bianca actually *approached* him about this? Had she tried to talk Ben into participating in the charade she had proposed to Kate earlier? It was hard to believe even Bianca could be that tactless, so Kate decided to proceed with caution. "What, exactly, did Bianca tell you?"

"She told me she had a plan to get you married, or to make it look like you were getting married, so your father will okay her own marriage."

That was it.

She'd kill her. She'd march right home, find Bianca wherever she was, and hang her from the highest rafter in the house by her toes. "Get me married?" she repeated stupidly, trying to sound as if this was the first time she was hearing of such a preposterous plan.

"It's okay, I know it was a desperate plan. And, for what it's worth, I think it's as stupid as you do."

The moments that followed seemed to last an eternity. What could Kate say? Admit to it and look like a fool? Or deny it and, potentially, look like an even bigger fool, given that Bianca had apparently spilled her guts as far as her grand plan went.

"It's not entirely Bianca's fault," she said in what she hoped was a casual voice. "It's our father. He's just so old-fashioned and Bianca is such a people-pleaser." She laughed as if she thought it was truly endearing. "The two of them are quite a pair."

Inside, she seethed.

"A determined pair," Ben commented.

Her smile froze. "What do you mean?"

"I mean, your sister is serious about this. Whether your father's ideas are stupid or old-fashioned or not, she's moving forward with her plan and if it isn't with me, she's going to move on and find another guy."

Kate had a mental picture of her sister—her own flesh and blood!—going from one single, divorced or widowed man to the next in Stratford, begging each of them to *please* take her spinster sister on a date.

The idea was absolutely humiliating.

And, heaven help her, she knew Bianca was capable of it.

"But I have a suggestion," Ben continued. "An idea that might help you out."

Kate narrowed her eyes at him. "You do?"

"I do."

What could she do? She was desperate. It wouldn't hurt to just *listen* to what he had to say. Listening didn't automatically obligate her to go with it. "Okay, then, I'll bite. What's your suggestion?"

"You pretend to go out with me."

Kate took a moment to digest this. It was the second time in twenty-four hours someone had suggested she pretend to date someone else. In fact, it was the second time in twenty-four hours someone had suggested she pretend to date Ben Devere. And it was the second time in twenty-four hours that she bristled at the idea, though sitting here with the man was a lot different than contemplating doing it with the memory of the kid he'd been. "You're suggesting I give in to Bianca's idiotic idea?"

"I'm suggesting you *pretend* to."

"What good would that do?"

He shrugged his broad shoulders. "It would solve your problem, wouldn't it?"

"Maybe."

"Sure it would. She'd think you were doing what she suggested, so she'd move forward with her own wedding plans instead of spending all her time and energy scrounging up dates for you."

"Okay." She lowered her brow and looked at him with suspicion. "But what would it do for you?"

He glanced at her and one brow lifted over one dark eye. "Believe it or not, it would lift a problem or two off my back, as well."

"How?"

He shook his head. "Just, trust me, it would."

There was only one conclusion. "Do you actually have family harassing you about dating, too?"

He snapped his fingers and pointed at her. "You got it. So if everyone thought we were an item, it would solve both our problems and, hey, it's not like either one of us have any illusions about romance or anything. At least not where each other is concerned."

Kate considered it for a moment. "That's true."

"So what do you say?"

Something told her this was a bad idea. She just couldn't figure out *why*. After all, she had better things to do than to argue with Bianca day in and day out about whether or not she should get married just to clear the way for Bianca and Victor. On the surface it seemed simple: if Bianca thought Kate was dating someone, especially someone Bianca herself had set her up with, there was no way in the world she would try to push her into a fake marriage with someone else. Bianca could plan her own wedding and by the time she learned Kate and Ben weren't really an item, it wouldn't matter anyway and she could go ahead and marry Victor.

Which meant Kate would save a lot of time, and frankly, a lot of guilt, *not* having to fight with Bianca.

On the surface, this was an idea that could work.

But when she looked over at Ben, she didn't feel the relief that such a solution should provide, but instead she felt even more tremulous trepidation, despite the kindness he'd just displayed in helping her with Sierra.

"I don't think it will work," she said at last.

He looked surprised. "Have you got a better plan?"

"No, but…it's just too crazy. Who'd believe you and I were actually involved suddenly, after all these years? It's—" she threw her hands in the air "—it's just so unlikely."

"All right…"

"No, I don't mean *you*." But she did. "I just mean *us*. I mean, people who've known each other as long as we have, and gotten along as badly as we have, don't suddenly fall for each other. No one's going to buy this."

"Well, you're not, and I'm not—"

"No."

"—but maybe Bianca."

"Ah." That was a point. That was a good point. "Maybe Bianca. You're right."

"And isn't that who you're looking to convince?"

"Well—"

"Look, I assume you're going to the charity ball at the country club tomorrow, right?"

"Y-yes."

"Me, too. So why don't we just go together?"

He looked so earnest when he asked it that it made Kate feel as if she would actually hurt his feelings if she refused. And making her first thought, *Yes, why not?*

But she had a hundred answers to that. This man who acted so kind and understanding was the same person who had been so ruthlessly insensitive to her when she was younger.

Kate was a firm believer that people didn't really change that significantly, at least not in terms of character, from what they were as a child.

And Ben Devere had been one wild child, she reminded herself as he stopped the car.

"I can't, Ben. But thanks for the suggestion. I really do appreciate it." She gave a brief smile and went on, "I really have to be going now. Good luck with your colt."

Without listening for an answer, she got out and began to walk away, but he came after her, grabbing her by the arm and turning her back to face him. For a moment, there was something in his eyes that she couldn't quite read, though it looked for all the world like pleading. "Wait a minute, what's wrong? Did I offend you?"

"Not at all. I just don't think it will work, that's all. I'll have to take my chances with Bianca and Victor and whatever plan they hatch up next."

He shrugged and shook his head. "The offer stands, if you change your mind."

"Thanks, Ben." Why did she keep feeling as though she wanted to take him up on it? What was *wrong* with her? She knew this guy was no match for her, not even a pretend one. So why was she entertaining this proposition at all? She cleared her throat. "I guess I'll see you at the club tomorrow night."

He nodded. "I'll be there."

"Okay, then." She took a few steps away, then hesitated and turned back.

But he wasn't looking at her anymore. He had moved away and was leaning against the paddock fence, looking off into the distance, and it looked as if he was a million miles away. She watched his straight profile for a long moment, trying to figure out what was behind that still expression, what was inside those piercing dark eyes.

But all she could see was a man alone, which was exactly what he'd always been.

She'd never really known Ben Devere and, clearly, she never really would.

Chapter Five

"I'll drop you girls off at the front door," Henry Gregory said to his daughters. "That rain this afternoon made a muddy mess of everything. I don't want you getting your pretty dresses ruined."

"Thanks, Daddy." Bianca leaned forward in a cloud of taffeta and kissed her father's cheek.

He accepted her kiss then glanced at Kate. "What, no kiss for your old man?"

Kate laughed and leaned toward him herself, her modest black satin shift creating considerably less of an obstacle. "Thank you for the ride," she said, kissing him. "And thank you for giving me a ride home early, too."

"Now, Katie, you just see if you're having a good time before you start talking about leaving, would you? Your mother absolutely loved these events. And she'd be so proud if she could see the two of you now." His voice tremored a little bit when he spoke of his late wife, and Kate was struck by how much it affected him in his daily life still, even twenty years later.

Then again, her mother was never all that far from her own thoughts, either.

Bianca got out of the car and Kate followed. "See you in there, Dad," she said, and nodded at the doorman as she passed, even though he was still watching Bianca walk away.

It was ever the case.

It was a typical charity ball, with lots of fosty older folks and music that wasn't quite classic yet wasn't remotely modern. Still, Kate had always loved the atmosphere at the Avon Lake Country Club, so it wasn't that much of a hardship to be here.

"Kate? Katie!" Bianca called, an hour into the evening, interrupting Kate's conversation with the eccentric retired professor from Avon College, Dr. Will Stratford, who was here to say a few words about the history of Avon. She rushed breathlessly up to the two of them. "Oh! Hi, Dr. Will."

For Pete's sake, did Bianca have to flirt with *everyone?*

"If it isn't the lovely Bianca," he said, patting his chest pocket. "That is, I *think* it's the lovely Bianca. Now, where did I put my glasses?"

"Oh, Dr. Will, you are too much!" Bianca turned to Kate. "Katie, there's someone you just *have* to meet. Dr. Will, would you excuse us for just a few minutes?"

He nodded, still checking his pockets. "Delightful to share your company, as always."

"What are you doing?" Kate asked in a harsh whisper, wrenching her arm free of Bianca's tight grasp. "We were having a really interesting conversation about the ancient Mayan culture."

Bianca rolled her eyes. "Lord above, I don't see how you're ever going to get a date, much less marry someone."

"I don't have any intention of marrying anyone."

"Tell me about it."

Kate searched the room and spotted her father by the opposite wall, talking to Margie Devere, Ben's mother, and another woman. She tried to catch his eye but he was deep in conversation.

But Bianca probably wouldn't notice that. She never wore her glasses and she hated contacts so, as a result, her far vision was very blurry.

"Dad's over there calling me," Kate told her. "Looks like he needs help extricating himself from a conversation."

Bianca squinted in the direction Kate had indicated. "He looks pretty happy to me."

"How can you see that far?"

"I've got contacts in. Now—" she took Kate's arm "—I'd like you to meet someone *very* interesting." They walked up behind a man and Bianca tapped him on the shoulder. "Harold?"

The man turned around and took an uncertain step. The short glass of bourbon he held in his hand probably explained that. "Yes?"

"Remember I told you I was going to introduce you to my sister? Well, here she is. Harold Dwight, this is Kate Gregory. Kate, this is Harold. He's *extremely* smart. In fact, he's writing a book on horticulture."

"Actually, it's about arachnids," he said, sipping his drink and blowing out breath that, along with a single match, would probably cause an explosion. His blue eyes were watery and reddened, an effect heightened by his straight red hair.

"Yes," Bianca said blankly. "Arachnids."

"Spiders," Kate told her dryly.

"It's a novel," Harold added.

Kate raised an eyebrow at her sister.

"A love story," he finished. "All about Danny, the lonely Daddy Long Legs who longs for true love with Wendy the Black Widow, even though it's dangerous—"

"Excuse me," a deep voice said at Kate's left shoulder.

She knew before she even turned around that the voice was that of Ben Devere, and she'd never been so glad for an interruption in her life, regardless of the source.

He smiled when she turned and met his eyes. "Didn't you promise me a dance, Kate?"

"A d—?"

"They're playing our song."

She listened. The band was playing Engelbert Humperdinck's "Release Me." She had to laugh. "Why, yes, they are. I was just thinking that."

Ben put an arm around her waist to guide her onto the dance floor. "Excuse us, please," he said to a glowering Bianca and a befuddled Harold Dwight.

"Was that Bianca's new target?" he asked with a smile as they glided to the opposite side of the dance floor, as far from Bianca and Harold as they could get.

"I'm afraid so."

"Hmm." He looked back in their direction. "I hope you didn't mind me taking you from him."

Kate narrowed her eyes at him. "No, that's fine."

"Are you sure? Because if you're not, I could just take you back over there with apologies and—" He started to lead her in that direction.

"No, *thank you*." Kate stepped on his foot. "Oh, gee, I'm so *terribly* sorry!"

Now it was his turn to narrow his eyes. "I'm sure you are." He tightened his arm around her waist, pulling her closer against his powerfully muscled body.

It was like leaning against a wall of rock.

"You know, a lot of people would think you would be grateful to me for offering you a way out of this. But not you. Katherine Gregory is grateful to no man."

"That's not true," she said sharply. "But I'm still trying to figure out what you get out of the deal you proposed."

"Because Katherine Gregory also *trusts* no man."

"You got *that* right. At least in this case. That reminds me, what ever happened to your pal, Lou Parker?" She watched him for a reaction.

He gave a laugh. "Last I heard he was in jail for insider trading. Why are you changing the subject?"

She raised an eyebrow. "A girl's got to be cautious about you, Ben Devere, despite your heroic actions of yesterday," she hastened to add.

"Have I ever given you reason not to trust me?"

"Are you *kidding* me?" She stopped dancing and stood in front of him on the dance floor, glaring at him. "Do you remember the time you held that lit firecracker under my nose and threatened to drop it down my shirt?"

"I was twelve!" he argued, adjusting his hold on her and moving her out into the middle of the floor. "And I didn't do it, did I?"

"No, instead you threw it five yards away and scared my horse half to death."

He did at least have the grace to look chagrined. "That was an accident."

"That wasn't an *accident*, Ben. An *accident* is something that happens *accidentally*. You *threw* the firecracker."

"Okay, then it was a mistake." He glanced around. "You know, people are starting to stare."

She didn't care. "Let them!" She was on a roll. She stopped again and put her hands on her hips. "What about the time you pulled my skirt up on Halloween so everyone at the party saw my underpants?"

He laughed outright. "That was second grade! Come on, Kate, you're going to have to do a lot better than that if you want to make your point. And—" he grasped her arm and led her none too gently toward the French doors to the terrace "—you're going to have to do it outside so we don't have an audience."

She wrenched her arm free before they got to the door. "You can't manhandle me this way."

"Manhandle? Honestly, Kate, it's like you're living in a nineteenth-century novel."

"Kate!" It was Bianca, interrupting again, but this time her voice was a little sharper and a lot less patient. She was hurrying forward with another hapless victim, this time a young blond man who couldn't have been over twenty-one.

In fact, he might not have been over eighteen.

"Kate, I have someone I want you to meet."

Oh, no.

This just wasn't going to end. Bianca had gotten this idea into her head and she was going to hammer away at it until…until what? Until Kate was dead or married, that's what.

She'd seen her sister determined like this before, and she just didn't stop until she got what she wanted.

Now, Kate could have tried to ignore it. But she knew Bianca would keep persisting, to everyone's embarrassment.

Ben Devere was an example of just how far afield Bianca would go with her plans.

Unfortunately he was also Kate's best hope for a reprieve from Bianca's plan.

And he knew it.

"Kate," Bianca said, dragging Kate away from Ben with a cursory nod.

"Bianca," Kate said, wrenching her arm free. She glanced back at Ben, who laughed and shook his head.

"Katie," Bianca went on. "This is Perry."

"Penry," the kid said.

"Oh. I mean Penry," Bianca corrected.

"No," the kid said. "Perry Penry." He held a shaking hand out to Kate. "Bianca told me you wanted to meet a younger man and maybe," he paused and practically circled his toe in the dirt. If there had been dirt underfoot, that is. "Maybe get something going."

Kate fumed at Bianca, feeling as if there might actually be fire coming from her nostrils. "*Bianca* told you you might be able to *get something going* with me?"

"Shh!" Bianca said. "Daddy's right over there. Don't let him hear you bickering."

"You have really gone too far," Kate said heatedly. Then to the kid, she said, "No, Penry—"

"Perry."

"—I don't want to start anything. With you or with anyone. And you'd best return to your parents, lest they should hear what you've been up to."

It was a gamble. She had no idea who his parents were or if they were even there.

Fortunately it was a gamble that paid off. The

boy went red in the face before turning tail and running.

When he was gone, Kate said to Bianca, "That was really too much. You've gone too far this time."

Bianca sighed. "I might have tried a wee bit too hard on that one," she agreed.

"A *wee* bit? You told that kid that I wanted to have an affair with him!"

"Well." Bianca shrugged. "Like I said, maybe that was a little bit too much."

"It was *way* too much."

Bianca nodded thoughtfully. "Next time I'll be more subtle."

"No," Kate said quickly. "No *next time.* There better not *be* a next time."

"There *has* to be." Bianca looked at Kate with pleading eyes, the color of blue candy. "It's my only hope!"

This was it. Time for Kate to make a decision that *could* affect the rest of everyone's life. Certainly it would affect the rest of the month, and maybe the rest of the year.

Absolutely it would affect what Bianca did about her own future with Victor.

"Stop trying to find men for me," Kate said, thinking fast. She said the only thing that came to her, the only thing that might help her get Bianca off her back once and for all. "I've already found one and you're going to ruin it if you keep interfering."

Bianca's jaw dropped. "You *did?* You already found someone?"

"Yes, I did."

"Who? Someone I know? Did you tell Daddy? How serious is it? Tell me *all about it.*"

"I don't want to talk about it yet," Kate said, hoping the cagey approach would work with Bianca this time. "I don't want to jinx it or anything."

It didn't work. Bianca narrowed her eyes. "You are totally lying to me."

"I am not!"

"Yes, you are. There is no man. You just want to get me off your back."

"That is *not true,*" Kate objected, but it was a somewhat feeble objection, considering the fact that what Bianca was saying was actually true.

"Oh, no? Then tell me who he is."

"What is this, some kind of test?"

"Yes." Bianca's angelic features grew sharp. "That's exactly what it is. Who is he?"

It was another moment of decision. A moment in which she had to make a choice to either follow-through whole-heartedly with this stupid plan, or 'fess up to Bianca and let her know, in no uncertain terms, that there was no way in the world she was going to maintain such a stupid charade just so Bianca would leave her alone.

A moment passed.

Then another moment.

Finally, Kate said, "It's Ben Devere."

Bianca's face split into a delighted and incredulous smile. *What? Ben Devere?*

"Yes." The words tasted strange on her tongue. "It's Ben Devere."

"I had no idea!"

Now that was a lie right there, considering the fact that Bianca had already approached both Ben and Kate about this.

"Well, it's true," Kate said, through the gritted teeth of a false smile. "I'm not saying there's any guarantee that anything's going to come of it. After all, it's been years since I last saw him and we're only just getting to know each other again now..."

"But you're interested?" Bianca asked excitedly. "Seriously?"

"Yes," Kate said in a firm voice. "Yes, I'm interested."

"Oh, that is *so cool!*" As she spoke, another nerdy-looking man—this one about mid-thirties with hair that looked as though it hadn't been washed in months—approached. "Never mind," she said lightly to him. "She's already taken."

Kate watched the man go, and turned her narrowed eyes on Bianca. "Tell me you weren't going to try to set me up with that one, too."

"He's *smart!*" Bianca said, trying to defend her position. "He's in, like, his seventh year of college."

Kate glanced in the guy's direction as he slinked away and joined two older, and equally unkempt, people whom she assumed might well be his parents.

"Okay, look," she said, dragging her attention back to Bianca. "You suggested I talk to Ben, so I did. And, surprise surprise, we actually have a lot in common. But if you keep dragging other men up to me—especially while I'm with him—you are going to blow the whole thing for me. So will you lay off?"

"Sure!"

"No, Bianca, I mean it." She held her hand out. "Pinky swear." Bianca was weirdly superstitious about pinky-swearing. She never, ever told a lie under a pinky swear.

After just a moment's hesitation, she locked pinkies with Kate. "Okay, I swear. I'll leave you alone. As long as you're interested in Ben," she hastened to add.

"I have a feeling Ben and I are in it for the long haul," Kate said to Bianca in a voice so unconvincing that it would require all of Bianca's blind hopes for her to believe it.

She did. "I'm *sure* you are!"

Across the room, Kate spotted Ben—dashing in his black tux and longish dark hair curling over the collar—talking to that loosey-goosey Penelope Finnegan. They looked quite interested in what each other was saying.

It irked Kate.

How dare he choose now, of all times, to look all hot and heavy with the town tramp?

"Is that Penelope Finnegan?" Bianca asked, squinting her eyes in their direction.

"He's giving her reference for one of his old trainers," Kate said quickly, wishing she could lie better when on the spot.

"Oh." Bianca nodded. Evidently it was convincing enough for her. "Well, you'd better go run some interference, because he doesn't look that interested in Penelope but she *definitely* has her eye on him."

Kate was glad to see distraction in the form of Emmaline Benedict. She flagged the brunette down. "Emmaline! Where is your new husband?"

Emmaline smiled and pointed to a tall, dark-haired man talking to a young man. "There's Ryan," Emmaline said. "Talking shop with Crispin Locke, the head of the computer department from the college." She shook her head. "He's a tech junkie."

Kate laughed. "But a good-looking one."

Emmaline beamed. "I agree."

"So, how is the renovation over at the Texas Lights going? I passed it the other day and it looked great."

"We're getting close, but you know contractors. They say a month and it turns into four. Everyone says that about them, but I'm always amazed how the stereotype holds up."

Kate laughed. "You must be so eager to open the place."

"We are," Emmaline said, then held up crossed fingers. "I'm thinking a month or two now at the most. You'll have to come to the opening party, of course."

"I'd love to." From the corner of her eye, Kate saw Bianca approaching Ryan Benedict and the other man.

Emmaline followed her gaze and said, "Uh-oh. Your sister's at it again."

"At what?"

Emmaline lowered her voice. "She said she's got someone she'd like Crispin to meet. She wants to set him up on a date."

Kate groaned inwardly. If she didn't act fast, Bianca was going to embarrass her yet again. "That Bianca," she feigned a laugh, then said, "Oh, there's Ben Devere. Could you excuse me? There's something I need to talk to him about."

"Sure," Emmaline said. "It was great to see you again, Kate. I'll let you know when the hotel opening is."

"Do that. I can't wait, " Kate said, and meant it. Then she turned her attention to Ben and steeled herself for what she had to do.

Chapter Six

"Okay, you've got a deal," Kate said, walking up behind Ben.

He turned to her, surprised. "Excuse me?"

"No, no." She looked past him to Penelope Finnegan, a thin blonde wisp of a girl, "Excuse me. Penelope, would you mind if I stole him away for a minute?"

Penelope frowned. "And what if I do?"

"Then I guess you're out of luck."

The last thing in the world Ben wanted was to be in the middle of yet another scene caused by Kate. "I'll give you that information later, Penelope," he said, flashing the woman a smile.

"You won't forget?" She cooed in a way that he just *knew* got under Kate's skin.

It was hard to keep from chuckling. "I promise."

Penelope smiled at him, then, within the exact same moment, flashed Kate a look of sheer contempt. Then she sashayed away, swaying her considerable assets in the process.

"You can't do this, Kate," Ben said to her.

"Can't do what?"

"Run the show all the time."

She gave him an impatient look. "I don't know what you're talking about."

"Okay, specifically, you can't interrupt a conversation *I'm* having with someone else and just end it. You just took over the conversation, the hell with what anyone else wanted, and I don't like it."

She looked genuinely embarrassed. "I didn't mean to do that," she said with such sincerity in her voice that Ben felt bad for having been too harsh with her. "It's just that this is more important."

"What's more important?"

She looked around, as if afraid someone might hear what she said. "My problem with Bianca," she whispered urgently.

He laughed. He should have known better than to think she was genuinely contrite for any reasons other than her own selfish ones. "It may be more im-

portant to you, sweetheart, but it isn't more important to me." That was a lie, of course. He needed her
to move forward with the plan to placate Bianca as
much as she needed it. More, actually.

Because if Bianca was happy, Victor was happy
and Victor held the key to Fireflight.

Because, the truth was, if Bianca was happy, Victor was happy. And Victor, Ben knew, was the real
power behind what happened to Fireflight. Yet when
Ben had approached him about it a couple of weeks
ago on the phone, Victor had expressed concern
about selling Fireflight to the rival ranch without
the family's consent.

But Ben wasn't going to win her over to his side
by acting desperate for her cooperation. That would
swing the power in their relationship, and he didn't
want that. Women like Kate saw that kind of weakness and they pounced on it.

No, Kate would respond to disinterest better than
anything else. "As a matter of fact," he went on, "I
think my offer has just about expired." He made a
show of looking at his watch.

She rolled her eyes. "Oh, come *on,* Ben. An hour
ago you were all for it."

"An hour ago you had been less of a pain in my
backside. I shudder to think what it's going to be like
an hour from now."

She lifted her chin and looked as though she was about to say something, when she changed her mind. "How about a nice, cold beer?" she asked instead.

He raised an eyebrow. "Trying to ply me with alcohol?"

"Not at all, I'm just thirsty. I thought maybe you'd join me for a beer." She gave a casual shrug. "Then we could talk about this in a civilized manner." The smile that followed was so dazzling that even though Ben could see right through her, he was drawn to her enough to let this play out for a little bit longer. "But if you don't want to, that's fine. I'm sure Bianca can find someone else to join me." She smiled.

"What do you want, domestic or imported?"

"You choose." Her amber eyes were alight. She really was pretty attractive in her own holier-than-thou way. "I'll meet you outside, okay? Out on the terrace?"

He hesitated.

"Ben, please. Give a little."

"Okay, okay, you got it. I'll be right out."

She turned and left, walking away in a much more subtle—and much more alluring—way than Penelope Finnegan had just a few minutes earlier.

Kate Gregory had an air of just not giving a damn that he found incredibly sexy.

That hadn't always been the case. He could still

remember the nervous kid she'd been, always fearful of the worst happening, whether it was her father's horse losing at the track or the fireworks lighting the trees on fire. In grade school, she'd always been the kid who took her sweater with her everywhere in case there was a fire alarm and they had to go outdoors.

For a long time, Kate's entire personality had been defined by the things she was afraid of.

She hadn't been very sociable, either, preferring to help the teachers take care of the younger kids during recess rather than interacting with her own classmates.

Then, sometime late in high school, after Gregory Farms had enjoyed a few comfortable years of success, she had begun to bloom. Suddenly she had moved with confidence, spoken with authority. And though he'd always had a thing for her, at least a little, his interest had increased tenfold.

Once, at a party, he'd even worked up the nerve to kiss her. And what a kiss.

But the next day, Ben's pal Lou Parker had seen Kate with another guy. Someone a lot richer and more successful. Lou said she'd told him she was only fooling around with Ben until someone better came along and now he had.

It had hurt, but the worst of it was Ben couldn't

really blame her. No one ever thought he'd amount to anything. Hell, his own father had said that to him countless times.

He didn't like to think about those days.

"Here you go," the bartender said, a little loudly, and Ben realized it wasn't the first time the man had tried to get his attention.

"Oh, thanks." He slipped the guy a tip and took the beers. For a few disconcerting steps he felt like the kid he'd been when he left Avon Lake, feeling as though everyone was looking at him and disapproving of him.

Apparently, Kate wasn't the only one with childhood hang-ups.

But he was able to shake the feeling pretty quickly. After all, he reminded himself, there hadn't been that many people in this Podunk town that he'd been all that interested in impressing in the first place.

He found Kate at the far corner of the terrace. She'd taken off her shoes and was sitting on the stone wall, dangling her feet like a kid.

"Aren't you cold?" he asked, handing her a beer.

"I am a little, actually," she said, taking the drink and setting it next to her on the wall. "But my feet were absolutely *killing* me. It's not often I have to wear lady shoes, so when I do I always seem to get blisters."

He took off his coat and put it over her shoulders. "I can't fix your feet, but maybe this will help warm you up."

She looked into his eyes. "Thanks but now *you're* going to get cold."

"Worried about me?"

"No, I just don't want to hear you whining about it." She smiled.

"Then give the coat back."

She laughed. "I'll take my chances."

"Don't say I didn't give you a chance." He raised his beer bottle to her and said, "Cheers." He took a long sip, then glanced back inside. "Man, I hate these things," he said more to himself than to her.

"You do? Why?"

He looked back at her. "It's like childhood holiday dinners. There are a whole lot of grown-ups here that I'm supposed to know and talk to, but I'd really rather just be up in my room watching 'Gilligan's Island.' Or something."

"But you're a grown-up now," she said, smiling. "You're one of *them.* So theoretically you should be over the whole 'Gilligan's Island' thing."

He took another sip of his beer. "Didn't happen."

She sighed. "I know what you mean. I'd rather be watching TV and eating ice cream myself."

He eyed her. "What kind?"

She didn't have to ask what he meant. "Cookie dough."

He gave a nod. "That figures."

She drew herself up in mock indignance. "What do you mean, *that figures?* Are you saying I'm a cookie dough *type?"*

"I'm afraid so."

"So what are you? Ah, wait, don't tell me—vanilla."

He raised his beer bottle toward her. "Very good."

"Boring."

"Imaginative."

"How do you figure?"

He shrugged. "If you're eating cookie dough, the good stuff is all right there, obvious. The only good stuff is the cookie dough. But if you're eating vanilla…I don't know, it's all the same. So it's all good."

She frowned, then said, "I'm not sure I agree."

"Doesn't matter. I thought you had something urgent to talk to me about. What is it?"

"Oh." She looked down for a moment. "It was…you know…the plan."

"The plan?"

She looked at him hopefully. "The plan to make Bianca think we're dating."

"Oh, that." As if he'd forgotten. "What about it?"

"I think we should do it."

"I'm not so sure." He took another sip of his beer. "As you pointed out, there isn't much in it for me."

"And *you* pointed out that you had your reasons for wanting to do it." She was right on top of things. "Has something changed?"

"One or two things." Yeah, he'd gone over his father's estate some more and discovered the debt was higher than Ben had originally thought. The ranch could run maybe two more years before going completely belly-up, but if he wanted his mother to be able to buy a nice place for herself and live the kind of life she was accustomed to, he had to figure out a solution *now*.

Kate sighed. "I don't want to play games, Ben. What do you want? Money?"

He had to laugh. "What, are you calling me a gigolo?"

She looked so profoundly pained at the word that he quickly took it back.

"I'm kidding, Kate."

"Not funny."

"Maybe not. I apologize."

Her mouthed turned up just slightly at the edges. "So, are you going to do it?"

He made a show of pausing, trying to look as though he was really weighing his options. "Okay," he said, with a long sigh. "Fine. I never could resist a lady in distress."

She gave him a dry look. "Or out of it."

He smiled. "Very funny."

"So," she said, back to business. "What do we do next?"

He put his hands up. "Now, wait a minute, Kate, if we're going to do this, we have to lay a few ground rules."

She looked surprised. "Such as…?"

"Such as, I'm not doing this halfway. If I'm going to convince this town we're an item, I don't want it to look like we've changed our minds a day later just because you get a bee in your bonnet about something."

"My bonnet," she said crisply, "is completely bug free."

"Your bonnet is a veritable beehive."

She gave him a seething look. "Fine. As long as we're laying out conditions, I have one of my own."

"Go for it."

"This is *not* real. It's not going to *become* real. I figure Bianca will have her wedding planned inside a month, six weeks at the outside. Once she does, then we end it." She narrowed her eyes at him. "I don't want you getting any ideas about the two of us having an *actual* romantic relationship."

Now, that was insulting. It was when his old aunt Keely would offer him a bowl of raisins—which he hated—and then tell him not to be greedy and take too many.

He didn't want the damn raisins in the first place, and he didn't want Kate Gregory, either.

"Look, Kate, I don't have any desire whatsoever to turn this into something else. Believe it or not, I do actually have other options in that arena."

"There's another thing." She pointed at him. "No other options, as you call them, during the time we're doing this. I don't want the whole town thinking I'm being duped by my supposedly beloved Ben while he's making time with Penelope Finnegan in the hayloft after dark."

"I haven't been in the hayloft with a girl for years."

"Oh, my God, you've actually been in the hayloft with a girl? I was kidding."

"Hey, don't knock it till you've tried it."

She put her hands on her hips, all schoolmarmish. "You're maddening, you know that?"

"I've heard that."

"Well, it's true. I just wish I didn't need your help." She sighed dramatically. "But I do. So do we have a deal or not?"

He reminded himself of Fireflight and how quickly that could turn things around for his family.

He held out his hand. "We have a deal."

"Good." She took his hand in hers and shook firmly. "Now what?"

He'd already given this some thought, before they'd even started their bickering. "Well, we're in the perfect place to make a lot of people start talking about us real fast. Let's take advantage of it."

"How?"

"Come with me." He put his hand out and helped her off the wall. Then he led her to the center of the terrace. "Here. This ought to do it."

She frowned. "Ought to do what?"

"Give Bianca a good view of us."

"Bianca?" She followed his gaze toward the club, then looked back at him. "What are you talking about? You think she's spying on us or something?"

He nodded. "As soon as I suggested we go outside, I noticed she was watching us. She's at the door now, trying to look inconspicuous. Too bad her hair is so big you can see it even when she steps back."

Kate looked again and saw just a bit of Bianca's poofed-up blond hair by the edge of the French doors. She had to laugh. "She's always been bad at hide-and-seek."

"Tonight that's a good thing," Ben said. "Let's give her something to see."

Kate pulled back. "Now wait a minute—"

"Don't blow this now." He slipped his arm through hers and pulled her off the terrace and across the freshly cut grass. "We've got the perfect opportunity here."

Indeed they did. The full moon was riding above the trees, casting long shadows across the rolling lawns. In the misty distance the town lights of Avon Lake glowed like a Renaissance painting of heaven.

A cool breeze lifted and ruffled through Kate's long chestnut hair like fingers and she was the perfect picture of an angel.

It all added up to a very romantic-looking picture, emphasis on *looking*. There was no way he and Kate were ever really going to get together.

Still, if the night was a stage, he couldn't have set the scene better if he'd planned it.

"All right." He stopped and put his arms around her.

"Wait a minute," she said uncertainly. "Do you really think this is a good idea?"

He kept his eyes fastened on hers. "Yes."

"I'm not sure I'm comfortable with it."

"With what in particular?"

She sighed. "I don't like the idea of people here thinking I'm another one of your conquests."

"*Conquests?* I would hardly say I've had *conquests*."

"You've had plenty."

He shook his head. "Look, you can't have it both ways, Kate. Either we're going to convince people we're involved, at the risk of them drawing their own conclusions, or we're not. Which is it?"

She hesitated, looking at him uncertainly. The moonlight touching her skin gave her an ethereal look.

For a moment, he actually *wanted* to touch her.

"I don't know," she said, shrugging. "I guess I don't really have a choice."

There was a light tapping sound in the distance and Ben saw that Bianca had her face pressed against the glass panes of the door.

"Then now's our chance," he said very quietly, taking her hands in his and trying to turn her shrug into something that would look—to Bianca, ten yards away—like something much more tender.

"To do what?"

He bent close to her ear. "To prove to Bianca we're romantically involved." He touched her shoulder, fiddling with the fabric of her dress as if he didn't have a care in the world.

She took a step back. "I think standing here together in the moonlight is probably enough."

"Not if you're backing away from me."

"Oh." She took a tentative step forward. "Okay."

"And talking just isn't going to cut it. There's nothing romantic about talking." He bent and kissed her cheek. "Your father and my mother were talking when we left the room, did that look romantic to you?"

"That's different."

"I hope so." He put his hands back on her shoulders and rubbed his thumbs against her skin, looking into her eyes.

"I'm not sure I agreed to *this*," she said in a harsh whisper.

"Then come up with something better."

"I can't!"

"Then you're stuck with me." And she'd better not blow it for him.

"Heaven help me."

He tightened his grip on her shoulders, struggling to make it look intimate and not forceful. "Loosen up."

"I'm *trying*."

"Try harder." He kissed her cheek and ran his mouth along her jawline. "She's watching your reaction," he said against her skin, "make it good."

"This seems extreme," she squeaked, without moving.

"Good," he whispered, pulling her closer to him. "With any luck, we won't have to do it again." He trailed his fingertips lightly down her arms. Her skin was soft and smooth. He didn't think he'd ever touched such soft skin as hers.

His guess was that few men had.

Her breath came out in shallow gasps. "We are *absolutely*…not…doing…this…again."

He made a show of smiling down at her, as if she'd said something delightful. "Fine. Then do it now. Make this look romantic."

"I *am*."

He almost laughed. She couldn't have been more tense if she was working to disarm a bomb.

"Do you think she's gone yet?"

"Work with me, Kate." He cupped his hand to her face just as she started to look up toward the window. "If she sees you looking, she's going to know we're up to something."

"But maybe she's not there anymore."

"Maybe she is." He touched her hair, running his fingers through the ends. "Remember. We have the same goal."

"You're right, I know." She made a show of trying to smile at him. "Can you tell if she's still there?" she asked through gritted teeth.

He glanced at the door without moving his head. "Yes, and now Victor's with her." He could feel their eyes upon him.

"Oh, come on, now Victor's watching us, too?" She started to turn and he stopped her.

"Don't. They'll know we're on to them. It will cast doubt on everything."

Kate bristled. "Okay. But if I find out this is some kind of ruse, just to get—"

"To get what?" he asked incredulously. "A little makeout time with a surfboard?"

She stiffened instinctively, then apparently realized her mistake and tried to relax her muscles. "I resent that—"

The terrace door opened and he knew if he didn't do something quick, everyone inside would hear Kate's voice.

"Kate, shh. They're going to hear—"

"Don't tell me to *shh*—"

That was it. Though it was the last thing he felt like doing, it was the only thing he *could* do. He lowered his mouth to hers, to shut her up.

It wasn't bad.

Her mouth was warm and soft, her breath sweet. She responded to his kiss immediately, as if an instinct she didn't have time to outthink had kicked in.

That was a surprise. It had honestly not occurred to him that there might be anything pleasant about this.

He took his time, moving his lips across hers in a

leisurely fashion, all the while keeping his ears open for any more sounds from the doorway to the clubhouse.

He heard nothing, but he figured it was better to make it a good show than to cut it short.

He kissed her deeply, and at first she responded in kind.

Then she stiffened.

He pulled back slightly and said in a quiet voice, "You could act like you're more into this, Kate."

"And you could act like you're *less* into it," she returned.

"Quiet." He twined his fingers between hers, but she stood so ramrod-straight that he could have tied one end of a hammock to her. "Help me out here, sweetheart," he whispered while he pretended to nibble her earlobe. "We've got one chance here, get it?"

She hesitated, and he thought he could see the wheels turning. Finally she gave a small nod. "You're right. Let's do it."

"Good. Now look like you're enjoying yourself. This is looking more like sexual harassment than love." He lowered his lips to the curve of her neck.

"It's...not...love..." she breathed.

"No kidding," he said against her skin. "Now, but if you could possibly act like a warm-blooded woman, you might not ruin everything we're trying to achieve."

"Maybe *you* just don't warm my blood," she said haughtily, but her voice quivered at the end as he traced the curve between her breasts, not actually touching anything, yet suggesting everything.

He smiled at her response. "Sweetheart, I haven't even turned the burner on and you're boiling."

"You may not have turned the burner on, but I think the switch is poking me in the stomach." She put her fingertips to his chest and acted as if she were tracing playful little circles. She smiled at him beguilingly and added, "But I can fake it."

Man, she was pretty good, he had to admit it.

But he could play, too.

"Have you had to fake it a lot?"

She shook her head slowly, the look in her eyes so fiery that he thought for a moment he might have been wrong about her. "No, you're the first man I've had to fake it with." She reached up and ran her fingertips along his cheeks and into his hair.

He cupped his hands on her waist and held her steady, looking into her eyes. "Five minutes alone with me in your room and you'd be singing a different tune." He kissed her again, and this time she kissed back. They were head-to-head, tooth-to-tooth, tongue-to-tongue.

Then he heard the door shut, and knew that Bianca and Victor had gone on to more interesting pursuits. Hopefully they were satisfied that things out here between Kate and himself were what they seemed.

But instead of stopping right then, he took another moment to linger on Kate's mouth, enjoying her response to him. But Ben Devere was an honorable man, and even he wouldn't take so much as a kiss from a woman under false pretenses.

He pulled back. "That should do it."

"What?" Kate asked breathlessly. "What about making it look like we're having a tryst?"

A *tryst? Conquest?* Who used words like that today? "Bianca and Victor are gone."

"Are you sure?"

He glanced toward the door.

Nothing.

"I'm sure."

"Were we convincing enough, do you think?"

He smiled, and enjoyed the way her cheeks went pink when he did. "Well, now, I'm not so sure. Do you want to keep going?" he added slyly.

"I didn't want to go in the first place," she snapped in a loud whisper, then lowered her voice again. "I didn't have a choice."

"Honey, you *always* have a choice."

"Not this time, and you know it."

"I understand."

She lifted her chin and looked down her nose at him. "There was nothing more to it than that."

"I understand that, too." He gave a spike of laughter. "I just hope that you do."

"What? Are you suggesting I actually *enjoyed* that…that…charade?"

"There at the end, you didn't seem too miserable."

"That was the point, wasn't it? That I shouldn't look miserable while my supposed romantic interest mauled me in the name of romance?"

He laughed. "Now that you mention it, maybe a good, er, *mauling* is exactly what you need."

Her jaw dropped. "Ben Devere, how dare you insinuate something like that!"

He'd gotten to her.

He liked that.

"I've heard enough!" she said, tossing his jacket to him, striding purposefully away toward the country club, bare feet and all.

"See you later." He watched her go, practically breathing fire with every step, and he wondered if this was truly worth it.

Chapter Seven

That was disconcerting, Kate told herself as she pulled her shoes back on and marched back to the clubhouse with as much dignity as she could muster.

She knew Ben was watching her from behind and she didn't want to look as if he'd gotten to her too much. Heaven forbid she should trip and fall on her way back in.

Still, her knees *were* feeling slightly wobbly and she wasn't entirely sure it was anger that was making them that way.

When she got inside to the party, she felt as if all eyes were upon her. And in the case of Bianca and Victor, she was right.

"Katherine Gregory!" Bianca said, looking both delighted and surprised. "I cannot believe what I just witnessed!"

Kate assumed a puzzled look. "What?"

"You and Ben Devere out on the terrace, that's what." Bianca's eyes were positively alight. "You two were totally making out."

Kate realized she had a choice to make now. If she acknowledged it, there was always the possibility that Bianca would figure out it was a ruse. After all, Bianca wasn't stupid, just blinded by her determination.

On the other hand, if Kate denied it, chances were better that Bianca would buy it without as many questions.

"No, we weren't," she said calmly.

Bianca laughed. "Come *on,* Katie, who do you think you're fooling? Everyone saw!"

Everyone? "Everyone?" The plan was to get Bianca off her back, not to set every tongue in Avon Lake wagging.

"Yes, ask Victor!"

Kate sighed. "Ben and I were just talking out there, and I don't want you interfering or making more of it than it was, okay?"

"Okay!" Bianca laughed again. "Whatever you say."

She was playing into this perfectly.

"And for heaven's sake, don't go starting rumors about us!"

"Rumors about who?" The voice was Ben's, as were the hands Kate suddenly felt upon her shoulders.

Bianca looked at him, then back at Kate, then at Ben's hands, then back at Kate again.

She didn't need to say anything.

But that never stopped her before. "Nothing's going on between you two, huh?"

"Between who?" Ben moved his hands gently on Kate's shoulders, in a brilliantly acted gesture of familiar affection.

Kate felt her muscles melt under his touch. "Between you and me," she said, utterly without the vehemence she was going for. "I was just telling Bianca that you and I are just…" She paused one, two seconds, before finishing, "Friends."

"Now, Bianca," he said, his voice as smooth as melted chocolate. "Kate and I are just starting out here. We don't want the whole town talking about this."

"There's nothing to talk about." Kate turned, making him lose his grasp on her, and gave him a meaningful look. Why wasn't he picking up on her cues? If she was telling Bianca they were just friends, why was he trying to convince her there *was* something happening between them?

"Uh-oh." Bianca put a hand in front of her mouth. "Looks like I'm causing your first lovers' spat. I'd better leave before I really get someone into trouble." She winked. "'Bye, y'all."

She sashayed off, and Kate turned angrily to Ben. "*What* was *that?*"

"Your sister."

"I *mean*," she said with exaggerated patience, "just what were you trying to do? Couldn't you tell I was trying to act as if I was denying what was going on?"

"But nothing's going on."

"*I* know that, and *you* know that, but we don't want *Bianca* to know that."

He frowned. "So to that end, you decided to deny anything was going on?"

"Exactly."

"Hmm. Interesting tactic. But it makes me wonder…" He rubbed his chin. "Earlier, when you said that there was nothing *really* going on between you and me, and that there never would be—"

"I meant it," she snapped.

"How do I know that?"

"Because I just told you!"

"But you just told Bianca there was nothing going

on when you wanted her to believe there *was*." His dark eyes had a light in them that she thought was amusement. "Which means that when you say up, you mean down, and when you say never you mean now." He reached to her and cupped her face with his hand, running his thumb along her jawline. "So, is that what you're saying, Kate? That you want me now?"

The most angering thing about this was how much she liked his touch. It made it even harder to shake it off, but she had to. "Very funny, Ben." She stepped back and watched his hand go back to his side.

"Hey—" he splayed his arms "—I'm not trying to be funny, I'm just trying to figure out what you want."

She lifted her chin. "You know what I want."

His beautiful mouth curved into a devilish smile. "Me?"

"No!"

"Shh." He moved toward her, putting his finger to his lips. "People will hear and you will undo everything we've done tonight."

She glanced around them and saw that one or two people *did* appear to be looking in their direction. "I'm not sure that's such a bad idea," she whispered. "If it means *you* won't get the wrong idea."

He laughed, but there was an edge to it that she couldn't quite identify. "Relax, Kate. I'm just giving you a hard time. The only reason I said all of that to Bianca was because I also wanted to convince her we had a thing going on, and I figured if we both denied it, she might actually believe us." He shrugged. "So it was sort of a good cop, bad cop thing."

She sighed. This tangled deception was getting to be too much even for her to keep up with. "Next time, let's make sure we agree on our act in advance."

"Sure."

She looked at Bianca and Victor, slow-dancing so close on the dance floor that they might have been welded together. "Anyway, it did seem to work. Every time she can peel her gaze from her beloved, she looks over here at us and gives a smug smile."

"That's good."

Kate nodded, still watching Bianca and Victor. "Yes. Irritating, but good."

"So what do you think, should we dance? In a strictly professional sense, of course," he hastened to add. "I don't want us to *enjoy* dancing together, just to do it while Bianca's watching."

Kate had to smile. "It's probably a good idea." She held out her hand. "Lead on, McDuff."

He took her hand and swept her so quickly and firmly into his arms that it took her breath away.

The band began to play one of the first good songs they'd played all night—a ballad from the 40s, one of Kate's favorite songs—and the lights went low.

"This one is for all the lovers out there," the bandleader said in a mellow tone. "Especially Kate and Ben."

Kate stiffened. "What the—"

Ben clapped his hand over her mouth and pulled her closer so he could whisper in her ear. "Don't say it."

"Did you have something to do with this?" she whispered harshly.

"No, it had to be Bianca. I saw her talking to the guy earlier. We played right into her hand. I'm sorry."

"It's not your fault." Kate's face burned with embarrassment as she felt the eyes of so many of her neighbors upon her and Ben. "It's Bianca. I swear I'll kill her."

"What's the big deal?" Ben asked, turning her at the edge of the dance floor and leading back to the center. "She just had the band dedicate a song to us."

"She knows I hate to be the center of attention."

"But she loves it so much, she probably can't imagine you really don't like it. Think about it, this is just the sort of thing she'd love."

Kate nodded reluctantly. "That's true."

"And we've just spent a considerable amount of time and thought and energy trying to get her to think we're together."

"Yes, but just *her. Bianca.*"

He laughed and pulled her closer. "Don't worry, Kate," he said, close to her ear, so only she could hear him. "It's only temporary, then we have a magnificent, theatrical breakup."

"Promise?"

"I promise." His voice was low and husky, and Kate had the random thought that he'd probably uttered those same words, in that same voice, more than once in his life.

She could only imagine where they had gotten him.

"So tell me something, Ben," she said as they rounded the dance floor again. "Do you have a girlfriend?"

"Besides you, you mean?"

"Yes, besides me." She laughed. "Out there in the real world. You are only here temporarily, right?"

"Yeah, it's my plan to head back to Dallas as soon as I've straightened things out here for my mom."

"You're a good son."

He splayed his arms. "What can I say?"

"So…what do you do in Dallas?" It only then occurred to her that she didn't know the answer to that. She still thought of him as the rakehell kid he had been, as opposed to a grown man with a real job and a life somewhere else.

"I'm a defense attorney."

"An attorney?" It never would have occurred to her. "And criminal defense, no less! Are you serious?"

"Yes, I'm serious. Why?"

"Because you…I mean…" She stumbled over the words, suddenly realizing that she didn't know why it surprised her and she sure as heck didn't know how to make it sound less insulting. She decided, in the end, just to tell the truth. "You were such a wild kid. Such a troublemaker. If I'd had to bet you were going to end up on one side of the law, it probably would have been the *other* side."

He laughed outright, attracting the looks of several people. "You know, you are the first person to just come out and say that since I've been back here. But I'm sure you're not the first one to think it. I don't know why everyone thought I was so rotten."

"Because you were. You were always getting into trouble. Or causing trouble and not getting caught."

He groaned. "Oh, not the fireworks again."

"That and other things." She remembered their kiss so long ago, and her hopes, and his lack of interest.

"You just went stiff as a board," he commented, "what the hell are these *other things* you're referring to?"

She couldn't tell him. She couldn't admit that she'd had a crush on him and had been hurt that he hadn't reciprocated. It was too pathetic. She couldn't bear to have him think she'd spent all these years pining away for him, which she absolutely hadn't.

And she couldn't bear for him to think that she'd been chilly to him when they met up this time because of that past rejection, because, in part, she had.

So instead she dredged out the only memory she had of him that was uglier than his rejection. "Well, there was that time you shot your dog."

He stopped and pulled back, looking at her with such raw shock that she felt a chill run down her spine.

"Because he was rabid. That was the hardest thing I ever had to do. Did you think I just did it for fun?"

All the blood rushed from her face and went clear down her body, leaving an icy cold path behind. Of course. She should have known there was some sort of good explanation.

And her underestimation of his character had been terribly unfair.

"Oh, my goodness, Ben, I had no idea."

He looked at her incredulously for a moment, then just shook his head and walked away from her, leaving her standing alone on the dance floor.

She watched him walk away, wondering what on earth she should do. As angry as he'd looked, she knew it was a bad time to go after him to try and talk, but, given what she's just so callously accused him of, she didn't have any choice.

"Ben!" she called, running after him.

He didn't break his stride, he just kept going, right out the front entrance and into the night.

Kate stumbled when her high heels caught on the fringe of the Oriental carpeting in the entryway, so she stopped just long enough to take her shoes off, then she hiked up her dress and ran after him.

"Ben!" She ran out the door and down the steps into the grassy sweep of green lawn he was crossing to the parking lot. She threw her shoes into the grass and ran faster until finally she did catch up with him.

"Wait," she said breathlessly. "Hear me out."

He stopped and looked at her stonily in the moonlight. "I've heard enough."

"You don't understand." She swallowed and wished frantically, in that fraction of a second, that she could think of something reasonable to say.

"Really? What don't I understand?" He looked at

her expectantly. "Look, this isn't about the dog, this is about the fact that you have *always* believed the worst of me, just like everyone else in this damn town. But the fact that you *still* thought that, even though I thought we'd gotten to now be friends, really stinks."

He was right. What could she say?

He turned and started to walk away from her again.

"No, Ben, wait. Please." She went after him again, catching up to him on the painful gravel parking lot. *"Please."* She grabbed his jacket and he turned to face her.

"What do you want, Kate?" he asked, and every iota of warmth was gone from his voice.

"I want to apologize."

"Fine. Is that it?"

"Well…I guess—"

"Great. Apology accepted. Excuse me." He moved away from her again, but she grabbed his sleeve.

"I didn't always think you were such a jerk," she blurted stupidly. "I liked you once."

He gave a humorless spike of laughter. "Wow, that's charitable of you."

"What I mean is…" She swallowed and looked into his eyes. There was nothing there but disdain and she just couldn't make herself go on with the truth.

He probably wouldn't have been interested anyway, and she would have spent her secret for nothing.

He heaved a sigh and said, "I don't have time for this. It was nice seeing you again, Kate, let's make sure we do it again in ten years or so, okay?"

"But our plan," she interjected feebly. "What about our plan to fool Bianca?"

He looked at her and shook his head. "You are really a piece of work, you know that? Even when you hurt someone and apologize, it's just a means to your own end."

"That's not true—"

"Tell me something, do you *ever* think of anything or anyone other than yourself?"

"Of course I do!"

"Well, I haven't seen it." He dug his keys out of his pocket, and looked her up and down. "And to answer your question, the deal's off."

Chapter Eight

Kate stood on the gravel parking lot, sharp rocks cutting into the soles of her feet, and just watched him get into his Jeep and drive away. She watched his wheels spit out gravel as he accelerated onto the driveway, then she watched his taillights disappear into the night.

Now what was she going to do? Her pretend boy-friend had broken up with her.

She felt horrible.

As she walked back toward the club, she wondered why she had gone on and on about him agreeing to their plan. She'd known, even as she'd made the idiotic arguments, that she was saying the wrong thing. The problem was, she'd had to say *something* and that was all that came to mind. She'd sounded even more spoiled and selfish than he'd evidently already thought she was.

Of course it wasn't losing Ben's cooperation in her plan that was making her feel so bad. The poor guy had had to shoot a beloved pet to put it out of its misery, and she had—for *years*— labeled him a monster for it. The sad fact was, it must have been really difficult for him. When she played the scene back in her head, she could imagine that what she had interpreted to be a cold, emotionless face was probably actually an attempt to keep his emotions in check.

Lord, she felt bad.

What a jerk she'd been.

She stopped before getting to the door. She didn't want to go back in there. She hadn't exactly been in a partying mood to begin with, but now the last thing she wanted to do was to socialize or explain to Bianca where Ben had gone.

Besides, she was barefoot and she didn't want to go searching for her shoes in the dark.

So instead she took her cell phone out of her purse and called the local cab company, after which she text-messaged Bianca's phone to let her know she was leaving. Bianca would get the message later, when she couldn't come running out to try to question Kate on her departure.

Then she went to sit on a bench by the croquet yard, under an old oak tree. The moon was still fairly low in the sky and looked twice as big as usual, like something from an Art Deco greeting card. Under the right circumstances, it would have been incredibly romantic.

Not tonight, though.

Not for Kate.

She sighed and leaned back against the cold, hard wrought iron bench. She'd made such a mess of the night. As soon as she'd arrived she'd had a bad feeling that this was going to be a bust. Initially she'd assumed that was because she never particularly liked big social gatherings, but now she wondered if it was a premonition of some sort.

It was a long ten minutes before the cab finally arrived. She got into it and gave the driver her home address, then leaned back against the cool vinyl seats.

"You enjoy the party?" the driver, a wizened little man with a thatch of gray hair ringing his head, asked.

She looked up and saw him eyeing her expectantly in the rearview mirror.

"It was lovely," she answered automatically. "I'm sure they raised a lot of money for breast cancer research."

"Good cause," the man said, clearly in the mood to chitchat. "My wife had it. Survived. It's been seven years now." He rapped his knuckle on his head and added, "Knock wood."

Kate smiled at him. It *was* nice to hear a bit of good news. "That's wonderful."

The cab bumped over the gravely drive for a few minutes. The only sound was the static-filled sound of Journey on the radio.

Wonder who's sorry now?

Kate had the answer to that one. And she knew she needed to apologize to Ben again.

"Excuse me." She tapped on the window between herself and the driver. "I need to make a detour."

Ben sat in his car outside his parents' house, wondering what the hell he was doing here and how he was going to stay and finish what he'd started without going insane.

This was not where he wanted to be. This wasn't the life he wanted. He'd always hated the unreliability of it. Now his point was being proven at his mother's expense.

He didn't know how long he sat there, looking at the wide Texas sky. Maybe ten minutes, maybe two hours. But when the headlights showed up in his rearview mirror and the taxi cab pulled up behind his car, he was surprised out of his own thoughts.

He got out of his Jeep, blinded by the taxi's bright lights in his eyes.

His first thought was, Who the hell is this?

But his second thought, before she got out of the cab, was *Kate Gregory*.

Of course it was Kate. She wanted him to finish what he'd started with her. She had an agenda, and he was screwing it up by getting her mad and leaving.

But he'd had every right to leave. He wasn't obligated to her.

The fact that she'd been so completely wrong about what he'd done wasn't what bugged him so much. He'd found in the last few days that Kate was wrong about him a lot.

That didn't matter so much. Usually.

What mattered to him now was that she thought he was the kind of guy who would take a pet dog out back and shoot it just for kicks. Because he was bored and had nothing better to do.

Because he was cruel and couldn't think of a better manifestation of it that day.

No, it wasn't just the accusation that had shocked and upset him, it was her serious underestimation of his character.

"What do you want, Kate?"

"I came to apologize." She paid the cab and he sped off into the night, leaving the two of them alone.

"You already did that."

She straightened her back, lifted her chin and looked him right in the eye. "I came to do it again. And again. Until you believe me."

He shook his head and shifted his weight from one foot to the other. "It's not that I don't believe you. You'd have to be a really awful person to not be sorry after making an accusation like that. You're not a really awful person."

"Thank you." She looked uncertain.

"What you are is a really awful judge of character."

"Now wait a minute—"

He waved her objection away. "You made a lot of mistakes, Kate, but the worst one was being so all-fire sure you were right that you were willing to accuse someone of something like that, even when you *obviously* weren't sure you had the facts."

"But I *was* sure—"

He raised an eyebrow."

"—I was just…wrong."

He almost smiled. So did she. But he kept it in check. He couldn't let her off the hook that easily.

"Is that all you have to say?" he asked her after a moment.

"What else can I say?"

He shrugged. "I've long since stopped trying to figure you out."

She swallowed visibly and appeared to be searching for words.

It was then that he noticed she was barefoot.

Against his better judgment, he said, "Get in the car."

"What?"

"Get in the car," he repeated, gesturing toward his old Toyota. "I'll drive you home."

"You don't have to do that."

"You're barefoot, you're wearing an evening gown, you've got no coat, and clearly you've got no sense. You can't go traipsing through the pastures like that." He nodded toward the Jeep again. "Get in. Otherwise I'm going to feel guilty and I think you've given me enough to chew on tonight."

That did it. With an uncertain nod, she headed for his car. He didn't open the door for her and she didn't wait for him to. They just both got in, put their seat belts on, and looked straight ahead as they made the five-minute drive in chilling silence.

When he pulled up in front of the main house, Kate unfastened her seat belt and turned to him. "Again, Ben, I truly am sorry."

"Forget it."

"Does that mean we're back on?"

He looked at her and gave a laugh. "No, thanks." Somehow he'd find another way to save his family's ranch. He couldn't bow to Kate Gregory anymore, no matter what the stakes.

"Okay." She gave a small smile. "Well, thanks for the ride." She got out of the Jeep and he watched wordlessly as she lifted the hem of her dress and made her way to the front door.

He waited to make sure she got in and when he saw the door open and old Henry Gregory greet his daughter, he backed the Jeep up, made a three-point turn and started down the long dark driveway and headed back to the Devere Ranch.

That hadn't been easy, he thought, tightening his grip on the steering wheel. It should have been. He and Kate had almost always been at odds to some degree, all their lives.

How he could have spent even a moment—and really, it had only been a moment—imagining there could be a spark between them, he didn't know. It was plain to see he'd been without a woman for too long. He'd been working too hard. When he got back to Dallas, he'd have to make up for lost time.

He parked the Jeep at the house and went inside, turning the knob quietly, so as not to get the dogs barking and waking his mother.

So he was surprised to see his mother sitting on the sofa in the parlor, wrapped in her warm old robe, holding a steaming mug in both her hands.

"Benjamin, darling." She smiled warmly and moved the mug to one hand so she could gesture him in with the other. "Come on in here and talk to your old ma."

He went in and sat in his father's chair opposite the sofa. "What are you doing up, Ma? I thought Denny and Pearl brought you home ages ago." Denny had been the foreman of the ranch for as long as Ben could remember, and his wife Pearl had helped Margie run the house and keep the farm hands taken care of. Since Lyle Devere had died last year, Pearl and Denny had also helped take care of Margie, checking in on her regularly and driving her places at night, because her vision wasn't so good anymore.

"Oh, I've been home a little while," she said lightly. Then she looked at him more seriously. "I was proud of you tonight, son. I think everyone in town could see you've grown into a good man. For all your wild days, you are quite the capable and responsible fellow now. I appreciate everything you're doing to help me."

He shrugged. He didn't know what to say to that.

"I know your father made you feel like you'd

never live up to his expectations," his mother said. "That was his fault, not yours. You know that now, don't you?"

"Sure, Ma. He was a mean old son of a gun."

She didn't take offense. Instead she just gave a small smile and nodded. "He could be at times. He wanted what was best for you, he just went about it all wrong."

Ben didn't want to talk about this. "It's water under the bridge now," he said. "Let's forget it."

"Okay," his mother said deliberately. "Then tell me, what's this I hear about you and Katherine Gregory?"

He shook his head. Maybe they should talk about his father instead. It was a little more comfortable. "I don't know what you hear, but I can imagine so let me set you straight. There's nothing going on between Kate Gregory and me. Nothing."

She raised her pale eyebrows. "That's an awfully vehement denial, son. There've been times that I've lived to regret believing you when you sound like that."

He smiled and stood. He wasn't going to talk about this anymore. "Believe me, Ma, when there's someone you should know about, I will tell you the truth."

She gave a small, private smile. "I understand.

You just want to wait until the time is right. Until you're sure."

He sighed. "Something like that." He kissed the top of her head.

"Just remember, Benjamin." She raised an eyebrow and looked at him pointedly. "You must always assume the very best about people, and then let them prove you wrong if they're going to."

He smiled. It was his mother's most overused saying. "I will. Good night, Ma."

"Good night, darling."

"The Devere kid, eh?" Henry Gregory looked at his daughter skeptically. "What's the matter, didn't have the nerve to walk you to the door like a gentleman?"

"Come on, Dad, he just gave me a ride home."

Her father looked her over. "He drops a young lady off outside, with no shoes on her feet, no coat, and he can't even walk you to the door? I don't like it. His mother raised him better than that, I can tell you that much."

"After the way I treated him, he shouldn't even have driven me home," she said. "Besides, he did wait to make sure I got inside." She'd noticed the headlights hadn't moved until the front door was open.

"What do you mean, *after the way you treated him?*" her father asked, frowning. "What have you done? Katherine, have you driven yet *another* man away?"

Kate looked at her father, shocked. "I can't believe you would say such a thing!"

Henry Gregory's face crumbled immediately. "I'm sorry, Katie." He put his arm around her. "Come. Let's talk."

As she went with him, Kate remembered how her father had been before her mother's death. But it occurred to her for the first time now, walking into the big old family room with him, that Bianca probably didn't.

No wonder poor Bianca was so cowed by their father's old-fashioned ways. All she'd really known was the strict disciplinarian. She didn't know there was a heart of gold beneath that gruff exterior. When he said he would be disappointed in her if she married before her older sister did, she took it to mean he would disown her.

And she believed it.

No matter what Kate said, no matter whether Bianca knew in her heart that her father was all bluster, she just couldn't bring herself to do anything that would disappoint him.

Where Kate had taken over the serious, responsible role when their mother had died, Bianca—she realized now—had become a pleaser, always trying to make things right for her father. Kate had always felt Bianca had gotten through their mother's death without too much lasting effect, but that just wasn't true. It had changed her completely.

This realization brought great sadness for Kate. She'd been so impatient with Bianca, all the while not realizing how much she'd missed out on by not remembering their mother very well or the kinder, more patient man their father had been. She was shy and overly agreeable around Henry Gregory because that was the only way she thought she could win his approval.

Kate sat next to her father on the overstuffed sofa. "Bianca wants to marry Victor. I think you need to tell her she has your blessing."

He wagged a finger at her. "You know how I feel about that."

"Dad, you've got stupid old chauvinistic notions about it. It's not fair. Not to Bianca *or* to me. What difference does it make if I get married first or Bianca does? It's not as if her private life affects mine one way or the other."

"You'd be surprised," he said cryptically. "There are things in this world that you don't understand, my Kate. This is one of them." He sighed extravagantly and leaned back. "I'm not as inflexible as you might believe."

That was a surprise. "What are you saying?"

"That some old dogs can learn new tricks. Even when their pups don't think so."

"Dad, are you saying—"

Her father waved his hand at her. "Enough of that. Tell me about you and Ben Devere. There was talk, at the ball, that you two were —how did Bianca put it?—*hot and heavy* out on the back lawn."

"Well, we weren't."

"No?"

"We were just…talking." She looked into her father's eyes and thought about her sister's plight with him. "Okay, it may have been a little romantic."

"So it's true." He gave a smile that crinkled the lines around his eyes. "Margie said the same."

"Margie?" Kate repeated, trying to puzzle out who that was. "You mean, Mrs. Devere?"

He nodded.

"Mrs. Devere told you Ben and I were…" She searched for the word. *"Involved?"*

"What she said was that her son, Ben, had always been a little in love with you."

Kate's jaw dropped. "I don't think *that's* true."

He tipped his head from side to side. "It's what she said. She was glad the two of you seemed to be getting along so well outside. I have to confess, I felt the same way. But then when he brought you home…" He shook his head. "Very disappointing."

"Please believe me, Dad, it wasn't his fault. We had a little spat, and it was all my fault. After that, I didn't even want him to drive me home at all, but he insisted. He was an absolute gentleman."

Her father heaved a sigh and pulled her into his burly embrace. "You know, Katie, you and your sister and—well, you've made me think. Women today aren't like they were in my day. I think maybe I need to change my ideas a little bit."

She pulled back and looked at him cautiously. "What are you saying, Dad?"

"That perhaps—just *perhaps*—if you're involved with Ben Devere anyway, I could let Bianca begin to plan her wedding."

"Oh." It wasn't exactly what she'd been hoping he'd say, but for him it was a big concession. "I think that's very sensible," she said, trying not to spook him off by insisting he drop the part about Kate being involved with Ben.

He nodded. "It will make your sister very happy, don't you think?"

"Yes." She thought about how Bianca might react and she smiled. "It really will."

"Good." Henry slapped his hands down on his thighs and stood with a heave. "Then I'll tell her first thing in the morning."

"Wonderful!"

He reached his hand out and helped Kate up. "There's just one more thing."

"What's that?"

"Let's have the Deveres over for Sunday dinner sometime."

Kate raised her eyebrows. "The Deveres? Ben and Margie?"

"Sure. They've been our neighbors for forty years. It's time we started acting more like friends. Especially now that you and Ben are so close."

Kate nodded, frantically trying to think how she was going to handle this situation. "That should be nice," she said automatically. It would. It would be very nice. She'd work it out. Somehow she'd *have* to work it out.

"You've got it," Kate assured him without so much as an ounce of confidence.

He stopped and smiled back at his daughter. "You've always been a good girl. It just took the right man to come along and see what I see."

"Thanks, Dad." It wasn't much of a compliment, but it would have to do.

Especially since she had so many more pressing things on her mind now.

Like getting Ben back.

Not an easy task, considering she'd never had him.

Chapter Nine

The next morning was cool and misty again, and Kate shivered despite the light sweater she'd put on.

But it wasn't the weather that had her so chilled. It was the prospect of seeing Ben and wondering what they would say to each other.

His horse was running against Kate's Flight for a workout today, so she figured he'd be here to see it. He and Victor had been planning it for several days now and she doubted Ben would refuse to show up on the off chance Kate would be here.

She stood for a long time, waiting and listening, until finally she noticed a figure standing at the fence several yards away, watching the track alone.

It was Ben.

Had he seen her and purposely stood far away? Or should she approach him and pretend she hadn't been standing there waiting for him for the past half hour?

She decided on the latter.

"Hey," she said as casually as she could. "It's awfully early. What are you doing here?"

He turned to her and looked genuinely surprised. "Running a colt against yours." He gestured toward the source of thundering hooves. A beautiful bay Thoroughbred, running about a length and a half behind Kate's Flight.

"Oh," she said vaguely. "I didn't realize that was today."

He looked back at the track, suppressing a smile. "It's today."

"So how's he doing?"

"Not so great," Ben answered grimly. "As you can see."

"I'm sorry."

His jaw set in a hard line. "Not as sorry as I am."

She watched him for a moment, wondering what on earth she might be able to say to warm him up a little bit. Nothing sprang to mind. "So," she said at last. "I had an interesting talk with my father last night."

"Oh?" He didn't look at her.

"Yes. It seems he heard you are I are interested in each other and he's decided that's sufficient reason to let Bianca go ahead with her engagement."

Ben turned and looked at her, his chocolate-brown eyes cool, like coal. "My mother was under the same impression. It seems Bianca was a busy girl last night."

"Well, we contributed to that impression," Kate conceded. "As you may recall."

He nodded slowly. "I suppose we did. That was probably a mistake."

She bristled at that, though she could completely understand, and share to a certain degree, his point of view. "Still, it seems the mission is accomplished."

The horses pounded the turf toward them and slowed to a halt in front of where they stood. Victor camc over and patted Kate's Flight on the neck. "Looks like you'll make a good solid second," he said to Ben.

Ben's jaw tightened. "Looks like it."

"He's going wide at the turns, especially right before the stretch. That might shave a little off his time."

Ben nodded. "You mind working with him a little more?"

"Not at all. Keeps ol' K.F. in line." He patted the horse again, then said to the jockeys, "Take them around again. Ben, could you come with me? I want you to see what I mean."

"Sure." Ben jumped the fence and joined Victor.

"See ya, Kate," Victor said.

"'Bye." She stood, feeling awkward, as Ben walked wordlessly away from her.

"So, are you going to the livestock auction over in Lake Jackson tonight?" Victor asked Ben as they walked away.

"You bet. Denny's got his eye on a mare out there. He thinks she'd be a real good investment."

Their voices trailed off, leaving Kate behind with the nugget of an idea forming.

She had an idea how she might get Ben's attention again.

"I have to say, this is one of the strangest first dates I've ever been on. What do they do at a livestock auction anyway?"

Kate looked at the handsome but somewhat vacant young man who walked beside her to the barn and said, "Eric, this is not a date, remember?" Eric Lemmon had been an intern at the ranch briefly last summer, earning a college credit while learning the business end of ranching.

He had not been the sharpest pencil in the box, and Kate had had to work a lot of extra hours with him, so when she'd called to ask him for a favor in return he hadn't hesitated.

"I know it's not a date, Ms. Gregory, but it's supposed to look like one, right?"

"Yes. So call me Kate." She couldn't believe she was faking a date to win back another fake date. Her life was such a tangled web of deceit that she wasn't sure even she could figure it out at this point. "And remember, when I signal you, you can leave. I'll pretend like you made an inappropriate pass at me or something."

"Can you at least pretend I got to second base with you?" he asked with a white, movie star smile.

Oh, he was going to do quite nicely.

"You can pretend whatever you want," she said, smiling back. "Just don't go spreading rumors."

He made the motion of locking his lips and throwing away the key. If she'd actually been on a date with him, the gesture would have been cringe-worthy, but since he was just a great-looking kid who was, hopefully, going to make her look like less of a desperate loser in Ben's eyes, it was just fine.

As long as he didn't do it in front of Ben.

"As for what they do at a livestock auction," she said, stopping for a list at the door. "They auction livestock."

Ben's auction wasn't until close to the end. With an hour or so to kill, he decided to go back to his Jeep and catch up on some phone calls when he saw Kate and some young guy standing, awfully close to each other in the crowd.

Huh.

So she'd found someone else to replace him already. And why not? What they had wasn't personal, so it shouldn't have been difficult to find another male human being with a heartbeat to fill the role. Hell, it could have been Dr. Stratford for all she cared. Just as long as it was a man she could tell her father she was dating.

Though Dr. Stratford would have been a little bit of a stretch.

And, truth be told, so was this kid.

It wasn't that he was younger than she was, because the age difference probably wasn't more than four or five years. It was that the guy looked so…so stupid. There was no other word for it.

No one would believe she was involved with him. And while Ben could have sat back and just let her fall on her face, he *had* agreed to help her. And clearly she needed it.

So did he. For business reasons only, of course. Nothing more.

He watched Kate and her companion for a moment, and thought she'd glanced his way, but she didn't say anything and when he approached she was so busy telling the kid to leave that she didn't even notice Ben was there.

"How will you get home?" the kid asked.

"I can get home," she said coolly. "But I really think you'd better leave now."

"But—"

"Seriously, Eric, just go. I don't want to talk about it anymore."

The kid shrugged and left, muttering something about baseball as he passed Ben.

"Trouble?" Ben asked.

She whirled to face him, her amber eyes registering surprise when she saw it was Ben. "Oh! It's you! No, no trouble. Why do you ask?"

He gestured toward the kid who had just walked away. "I just overheard you and your…date?"

"No, no, no, that was no date. Though he certainly seemed to think it was." She shook her head, a wan smile playing at her lips. "Men."

"A couple of days ago, you needed one pretty badly."

She nodded. "That's true."

"Hmm." He stepped up beside her and didn't say anything else.

For a long time they stood there, side by side, not speaking. Ben was reasonably sure, however, that Kate was as aware of his proximity as he was of hers. The tension between them was almost palpable, but by the time he'd settled in and really noticed it, he was already there.

And he wasn't leaving.

They watched the auction wordlessly until, at last, the mare he'd come to bid on was brought up.

The auctioneer began to call the auction and Ben placed the first bid, for fifteen hundred dollars.

The second bid, however, went to Kate.

Kate?

"What the hell are you doing?" he asked.

She looked at him impassively, without so much a flicker of self-consciousness in her eyes. "Bidding on a mare, Ben. What the hell are you doing?"

"You know damn well I'm bidding on the same mare."

"Well." She turned back to the auction, leaving him her straight profile to talk to. "May the best woman win."

He couldn't just let it go at that. "Are you doing this on purpose?"

"Of course." The tiniest of smiles seemed to be playing at her lips. "Only an idiot bids at auction by accident."

"I mean," he said, "are you trying to outbid me?"

She raised her hand, raising the bidding to three thousand dollars. "Unless you're giving up, it seems I am."

He looked at her for a moment in utter disbelief, then turned back to the auction, which was racing toward four thousand dollars. He bid five thousand and turned back to her. "Can you leave it at that?"

"Can you?" she asked. "Because I want the mare." She raised her hand, winning the bid at five thousand, two hundred and fifty dollars.

Ben couldn't believe it. "Stop it."

She raised her hand, then turned to him. "You."

"I can't. I need the mare."

"So do I."

"How could you possibly need *this* mare, of all the horses that are up for auction tonight? Of all the horses you already have!"

She shrugged. "Victor told me she was a good buy." It was true, but it was only after she'd asked Victor why Ben was coming.

"Well, she's not."

"Then why are you bidding?" She raised her hand again. She could do this all night.

He put his hand on her forearm to hold it down. "Stop it, you're just driving my price up."

She looked at him. "*You're* driving *my* price up."

He shook his head. "You're a real pain in the ass, you know that?"

"I've heard it." She smirked. "But I don't believe it."

"Well, believe it." He raised his hand to up the bid, then looked back at her. "So what does it take to get you out of this bidding war?"

"I don't know. Maybe…" She looked back at the horse and the auctioneer. It really was a beautiful mare, there was no doubt about it. She had little to lose by bidding. "Maybe you agree to help me help Bianca and Victor again?"

He frowned, thinking.

The auctioneer tried to raise the bid.

Kate tapped her fingers. "I'm ready to raise the bid," she taunted. "I've got a long way to go."

Ben rolled his eyes. "How long?"

The auctioneer's voice interjected, *"Going once…"*

"Probably longer than you."

"Going twice."

Ben looked at the mare, then the auctioneer, then

Kate. She wasn't kidding. She wanted what she wanted and she was ready to go as far as she needed to, to get it.

"Okay, I'll do it," Ben said to Kate, and he gestured to the auctioneer.

"Sold! To the man in the blue shirt..."

"Good choice," Kate said lightly.

Ben smiled. He almost had to respect her boldness in business. If he hadn't been the one to suffer for it, he'd have respected it a lot. "What, the mare?"

"Her, too." Kate smiled and looked at the auction block. She knew he hadn't just chosen the mare, he'd chosen to help Kate, and that was all that really mattered to her at this point, regardless of how much Victor wanted the horse.

Right now all that mattered to Kate was that she'd won Ben over and had him back on her side.

And she did.

Mission accomplished.

Chapter Ten

Ben won the auction, for about two thousand dollars more than he'd intended to spend.

But at least he'd gotten the mare.

She, along with Fireflight, could bring the Devere Ranch back into play.

After checking in with the auction staff, he returned to Kate and said, "I assumed that, in light of what you told me this morning, you were laying our plan to rest?"

She raised her chin for a moment, then looked as if she'd changed her mind about whatever she was going to say. "No, actually. The truth is, I need you

now more than ever. But I understand why you're reluctant to help me."

"Then why the strong-arming?" He gestured toward the auction block. "Why bid against me until
I agreed to your plan if you understood why I might
not want to help?"

She looked pained for a moment, then said, "That
probably wasn't fair." She turned her amber gaze on
him and said, "I'm sorry. We did want the horse, but
maybe not as much as you did. I should have talked
to you up front."

Ben was surprised. He'd never heard Kate Gregory admit to any sort of wrongdoing whatsoever.

He hesitated, then mentally crunched his pride
into a ball and tossed it away. "Listen…can we talk
privately for a moment?"

She nodded. "If you like." Then she looked hesitant and added, "Let's go outside."

"Fine." That suited him better anyway. Fewer po-
tential witnesses to him making a fool of himself.

They walked out into the balmy twilight and took
in the soft air. The first stars were starting to shine
in the sky.

"Is this private enough?" she asked, leading him
to the side of the large barn where the auction was
taking place. Despite the building looming behind
them, full of life and people, there was nothing left,

right or center, apart from rolling pastures and parked cars.

"It's fine," he said to her, then looked for some eloquent way to say what he had to, but settled, instead, for some plain talk. "Look, Kate…let's just forget what happened."

"Which part?" she asked, frowning.

He had to laugh. "The bad part."

She laughed, too. "Again, you're going to have to be more specific."

"You know what I'm talking about." He sobered. "Let's just finish what we started."

"Really?" She looked surprised.

He nodded. "No sense in us being childish about it."

"You're saying you're really willing to go through with our plan to help Bianca?"

"I guess I am."

She smiled broadly. "Are you sure?"

That was the $64,000 question. And the answer was no. He wasn't sure of anything where Kate Gregory was concerned.

No point in letting her know that, though.

"Of course I'm sure."

"Oh, Ben!" She threw her arms around him impulsively. "Thank you so much!"

For a fraction of a second he wasn't sure what to

do with his hands, but he decided pretty quickly to do what came naturally.

And what came naturally was to put his arms around her and pull her into a close embrace.

This is a mistake, a voice in his head objected.

A big mistake.

But who could resist?

Why stop now, when she made the first move?

There was no harm in having a little fun with her, was there? It wasn't as if it was going to lead to anything.

Kate hoped he'd kiss her.

Against all common sense, against everything she knew was right and proper, despite her resolve to resist him, she hoped he'd kiss her.

And he did.

The voice of her conscience objected strenuously. *Don't do it! This can't lead to anything but trouble!*

But her libido, long dormant, had the overruling vote.

This guy is far too sexy to ignore.

He lowered his mouth onto hers and scooped her into his arms, pulling her close against his body.

She couldn't think. She didn't even want to try. Instead she let go. Her muscles relaxed within his embrace, and she could only let herself immerse herself in the sensation.

It wasn't as if she'd let this go too far, she thought, trailing her hands slowly across the muscles of his back and across his shoulder blades.

Ben splayed his hands against her lower back, pressing her against him further. She felt the zipper and snap of his jeans against her stomach and tried not to think about taking things further.

He ran his tongue across her lower lip, then kissed her cheek, her chin and her jawline. She leaned her head back, basking in the sensuous tickle of his mouth against her throat.

This was nice.

She'd just give it another moment, then call a halt to it.

Ben kissed her mouth and for a moment she sank against him, her thoughts swirling like decadent temptations in her mind.

She wanted more.

And *that* would never do.

She pulled back. "Okay, I think we've got the routine down now."

He chuckled. "Honey, I don't think you know *half* the routine."

She had to resist sucking in her breath and imagining all those things she didn't know about his physical prowess.

It didn't bear thinking about.

"I know enough."

He put his hands up. "Okay, okay. Don't say I didn't offer."

"And what exactly—" she put her hands on her hips "—are you offering, Mr. Devere?"

He raised an eyebrow. "What are you hoping I'm offering, Miss Gregory?"

Oh, she had a lot of answers to that, none of which she wanted to reveal. "Very funny. What I hope," she said slowly, so that she could sound more serious than she felt, "is that you're not offering me some sort of…physical relationship. Because, as I believe we outlined in advance, that is out of the question."

"Oh, yes, we outlined that in advance. Paragraph four, line eight. I remember it well."

"Good." She inhaled a breath. "Then we should have no problems."

"Right. At least I don't. But you do."

"Oh?"

He nodded, his expression decidedly smug. "As far as I can tell, you're out a ride home tonight."

She'd sent Eric on his way so she could ask Ben for a ride if she needed to work on him more. Now that she didn't, she wasn't sure what to do.

Unfortunately her libido, or something very much like it, took over.

"Can you give me a ride?" she asked. "At least to your place so I can walk home from there?"

Ben laughed outright at that. "You think I'm going to take you to my place and have you traipse through the pastures? You already know I'm not that kind of guy."

She smiled. "Looks like I'm in luck, then."

He sighed and shook his head. "Looks like you are. Come on." He led her through the remaining crowd, stopping briefly to talk with Denny, his ranch foreman, about taking the mare home.

Then he put his arm on Kate's shoulder. "Looks like you've got yourself a deal now."

"And you're sticking with it?"

"Absolutely."

"It's all in the name of a worthy charity," she pointed out.

He shrugged. "Or good business."

"What?" That didn't make sense. "I'm doing this for Bianca. I mean, it's partly to get her off my back as far as setting me up with men goes, granted, but I also really want to help her out."

"I'm sure you do," he said, his expression unreadable. "This works for all of us, no doubt about it."

That stopped Kate. "What do you mean?"

He paused for a moment, then shrugged. "Not much. Just that you have your reasons for going through with this and I have mine. We both benefit, so what's the problem?"

She looked skeptical. "Nothing," she said, her voice extremely hesitant. "I suppose. Unless there's something you're not telling me, and I'm getting the distinct impression that there is."

"Come on, that's paranoia talking. All you need to worry about is whether this benefits you, and I think it does." They reached his Jeep and this time he opened the passenger door for her. "See? Nothing to worry about."

There was a lot to worry about, of course. Not until Bianca started planning her wedding to Victor could Ben really relax in the knowledge that he'd secured Fireflight for the Devere Ranch.

And by the time that happened, Kate would be off the hook, too.

So it worked out for everyone.

Didn't it?

The drive home was filled with small talk, about everything from the weather to the chances of the Dallas Cowboys making it into the Super Bowl. Kate didn't say one thing of importance, but her mind was racing with things she couldn't talk about.

The deal with Bianca, for instance.

The question of how they'd end this once it seemed safe to do so.

The question of when on earth it was going to seem safe to end it.

And about a thousand more.

They were almost at Kate's home when Ben asked, out of the blue, "Why aren't you married?"

"I beg your pardon?" Once again, she slipped into nineteenth-century mode. "Why are you asking me that?"

"Because you're beautiful, Kate, and you've got a lot to offer. I can't help but wonder why you need to have some guy—me, in this case—pretend to be your boyfriend."

She flushed under his praise while, at the same time, she cringed under his implication of her as spinster. "It's just the timing," she said, trying to sound light. "I wasn't seeing anyone at the moment, and Bianca and Victor wanted to get married, but Daddy's stupid old-fashioned views on that were putting the kibosh on things..."

He listened to everything she said, then, as if she hadn't spoken at all, asked again, "But why don't you have someone?"

The answer to that was long, complicated and a little bitter. "Have you looked around Avon Lake? There aren't a lot of bachelors here, and the ones that are here are either spoken for or, more likely, inappropriate."

"So you're doomed by geography."

"For the moment, yes. What about you?" she asked, hoping to turn the focus from her. "You're also unattached. Why? Is that any stranger than me being unattached?"

"Sure."

"How?" she asked irately. "Because I'm a woman?"

"No, because I'm a difficult son of a gun and it would take a special woman to tame that in me."

Even though he'd pulled up in front of her house, that one brief statement, that tiny sentence, raised so many questions in her that she didn't know where to begin. "So you're just this wild mustang, needing to be tamed by the right woman."

He looked for a moment as though he was going to disagree, but then he gave a single nod. "Yeah, that's me." He held back a smile, though. Kate just wasn't sure if he was laughing at the idea of himself as the wild mustang or at her for her naiveté.

"So who is this special woman? What is she like?" she asked, trying to sound jocular, but seriously wondering. "What does it take to tame a man like you?"

"Intelligence," he said quickly. "Sense of humor.

Sense of honor. Reasonably attractive." He gave a rakehell smile. "Someone sort of like you."

Kate swallowed, trying to decide whether this was a compliment or a huge insult.

Before she could respond to either possibility, he continued. "Like you, only without the attitude."

That got her. *"Attitude?* What are you talking about? I'm the most easygoing person I know!"

"Then you need to get around more."

She narrowed her eyes at him, shooting indignance through them, even as she wondered if he was right and why he felt that way about her. "I think I'll leave now." She started to open the door, but he caught her arm.

"Come on, now, Kate, can't you take a little ribbing?"

"Of course I can, I just have to get ready for the Daltons' party tonight."

Ugh, the Daltons' party. He'd forgotten about that. He did *not* want to go, but his mother was set on it and she'd insisted she needed him to escort her. Granted, he could cut out a few minutes after he got there, and come back to pick her up, but he still had to make an appearance and he was absolutely not in the mood for that.

Except now he knew Kate was going to be there.

That made things at least a little more interesting.

Especially since her reaction to his going would probably be amusing. "I'm going to that party, too," he said casually.

"*You're* going to the Daltons' party?"

"Sure. Why not?"

"Because it's the kind of thing you hate. Just like the charity ball at the country club."

Only without the good cause, he thought privately. "I'm in Rome. Got to do as the Romans do, I guess."

"Well, that's true, pretty much all of Avon Lake will be there."

He groaned inwardly. That did *not* make it more appealing. "You know we've got a golden opportunity to convince the community we're together. We ought to take advantage of that."

That was something she couldn't argue with. Especially since she didn't want *him* to question it at all. "I suppose you're right. But after tonight, with any luck, we'll be finished. Won't we?"

"Is it my imagination or is there—" she searched for a non-humiliating way to put it, just in case he disagreed "—something else going on between us?"

He took a long breath in before saying, "I don't know. Are you afraid there is? Is that what you're saying?"

It seemed as if he was being as cautious as she

felt, but she couldn't be sure. "I'm just asking the question, Ben. You don't have to answer based on what you think I feel."

"Are you sure? It seems to me I have to be damn careful what I say to you about something like this."

There was a long pause before she said, "I'm starting to think there's no way we're ever going to be able to be honest with each other."

"It takes a lot of trust."

"And a lot of confidence."

"Which neither of us can count on at the moment."

She looked straight ahead. "I suppose you're right. Except…"

"What?"

She started to speak, then changed her mind. "Forget it. I'll just see you at the party tonight. And, Ben—" she turned to face him as she opened the door "—thanks for everything. You've really been a huge help."

He looked embarrassed. "Don't mention it. Really. This works for all of us."

She got out of the Jeep wondering how this deal could possibly help him as much as it helped her.

Chapter Eleven

The Daltons' party was even more crowded than the country club charity ball had been, much to Ben's dismay. He was never one for socializing, but these large Avon Lake events had *always* been too much for him.

But he had to admit, being here with Kate, even if it was just for show, made it just a little more bearable.

It didn't hurt matters any that she looked gorgeous. Her chestnut hair was pulled back, showing off her large amber eyes. Unlike many of the women here, she didn't wear a lot of makeup, so her skin looked bare and touchable. As he watched her interacting with people as they went in, he couldn't help but feel an impulse to reach out and touch her. Yet at the same time, he enjoyed standing back and watching her smile, listening to her laugh.

He figured he must be pretty bored if he was that easily entertained by watching her.

He'd been feeling that way ever since he and Kate had gotten locked in the track shop. Of course, he wasn't about to admit that to her. He was barely able to admit it to himself.

"What are you looking at me like that for?" Kate asked when she turned away from a conversation with Dr. Stratford and faced Ben. As soon as she met his eyes, she looked surprised.

"Like what?"

"Like you've never seen me before."

Maybe he hadn't. She certainly seemed like a new person all of a sudden.

But—and he was reluctant to admit that—maybe it was he who had changed.

"Don't be ridiculous," he said to her. "I'm not looking at you any particular way."

She raised her eyebrows skeptically. "All right. If you say so."

He was eager to change the subject. "Is that Sheila Geshen over there? I thought she'd left town with her pool boy."

Kate looked and giggled. "She did. Now they're

back and he's going by the name Jose instead of Joe. They think no one will realize it's the same scandalous relationship. And of course no one says anything so they think they're getting away with it."

Ben smiled at how animated Kate got talking about it. "Scandalous relationships are usually the most exciting kind."

"At first," she agreed. "But ultimately I think you need to marry your best friend, and that's not usually scandalous." She looked into his eyes and suddenly it was she who was looking at *him* as if she'd never seen him before. "But if you have passion on top of friendship—" she swallowed and glanced away "—well, that's the best."

"Funny how it can take you by surprise sometimes," he said quietly. "One minute you're just friends, maybe not even that, and the next minute you realize you're in love."

"Do you think that really happens?" she asked, meeting his gaze again. "Do you think something like that can be real?"

He gave a short laugh. "If you'd asked me a couple of months ago, I would have said no, but now…" He shrugged. "I'm beginning to think it can."

"So am I."

A long, shivering moment passed between them before they were interrupted by Erin Dalton.

"Kate, I'm *so* glad you're here. You have *got* to see what Terrence did to the den. Remember the exposed beam he was trying to put up?"

"Y-yes." Kate glanced uncertainly between Ben and Erin.

Erin slipped her arm through Kate's and started to lead her away. "Well, it's been an absolute catastrophe, it is *such* a hoot." She looked back at Ben and said, "Excuse us a minute, would you? I promise I'll bring her right back."

Ben waved her off. "She's all yours."

He was still standing there, watching Kate walk away, when Bianca found him.

"It looks like things are going really well between you and Kate," she said in a singsong voice.

He was cautious about his answer. It was none of Bianca's business what really was, or wasn't, going on between himself and Kate. What did matter, where Bianca was concerned, was his mother's future.

"Does that mean you and Victor are ready to pony up, so to speak?" he asked Bianca.

She smiled. "As long as you convince Daddy you and Kate are really together, you've got it. Victor says we can spare a shot."

He wasn't sure what to say. He didn't like deceiving Kate's father. It was one thing to fool Bianca, since she was the one who had suggested the preposterous deal in the first place, but lying to Kate's father? He just wasn't comfortable with that.

Fortunately he didn't need to respond yet because Bianca kept talking. "It *does* seem like you and Kate are together," she said, looking at him with a sharp blue eye. "What's that all about?"

"Isn't that what you wanted?"

"Of course, it's just that…" She fluttered her hands in front of her. "I never dreamed you two would really hit it off."

Ben found himself looking around the room for Kate, wishing she would come back and save him from this awkward conversation.

"We did what you wanted," he said noncommittally.

"Yes, you did." Bianca beamed. "Now Victor and I can get married. Well, hopefully. I'll have to talk to Daddy tonight, but it's just a formality. Still, I owe you a big one." Then she shrugged and added, "But I guess you're getting something big in return, aren't you? Fireflight is quite the prize."

"So is Kate." Ben felt like he had to add. "For someone."

"Oh, of course!" Bianca nodded enthusiastically. "The only problem with Kate is that she marches to a *much* slower drummer than I do. That's why I had to ask you to step in and help."

Help. He turned the word over in his brain. It hadn't exactly felt to him as though he was courting Kate to help Bianca. As a matter of fact, it hadn't felt as though he was really *courting* Kate at all, only that he was chasing her down, constantly. She'd always been like a wild pony who was hard to catch, and hard to figure out.

But lately…well, something had changed.

"Anyway." Bianca bubbled on. "You did a *great* job. And you're an absolute *angel* for helping me out like this. Really."

Something about this didn't feel right. He was on the verge of telling Bianca that when she squealed, "Daddy!"

Henry Gregory had come up behind them. "Hello, my love." He kissed his daughter on the cheek. "I'd like to have a word with Mr. Devere in private."

"Oh? What about?"

"Never you mind," he said, and gave her a little push. "Run along now. Find something else to do. Go pester that fiancé of yours."

"Fiancé?" She beamed. "Does that mean we can *finally* set a date for the wedding?"

Henry Gregory gave a single nod. "Set your date," he said, then looked squarely at Ben, but said to her, "I don't see why you shouldn't at this point."

Ben looked straight back at the man in front of him. He wasn't afraid of him, though Henry Gregory had always been known as an intimidating man. What concerned him was the lie he had perpetrated against the man, even though it was for his mother's sake.

It was hard to regret doing everything he could to save her home for her.

"Come on into the library with me, son."

"All right."

Henry led the way down several corridors to the Daltons' large, high-ceilinged library.

They stepped in and Henry closed the door behind them. It shut with a dull thud, somehow emphasizing how alone the two men were together.

They moved over to tall, leather wing-backed chairs. Ben sat with his back to the door and Henry sat opposite him and leaned toward him to speak.

"I'll get right to the point," Henry said. "I'm confused about the conversation that you just had with my daughter."

"What are you confused about? What did you hear?"

Henry Gregory let out a long sigh. "I'm sure this isn't right, but it sounded just now like you were pretending to be in love with my Katherine in order to get some other kind of gain for yourself."

"No, that's not correct," Ben said. "I care for your daughter." He did. With every moment that passed he realized it more. "Very much. I would never do anything to hurt her. Especially not for my own personal gain."

Henry narrowed his brown eyes at him. "Can you give me your word on that?"

Ben nodded. "Absolutely."

"And you care for her. Very much. That's what you said."

"Yes."

"Then rather than participating in some scheme, I expect you'll be wanting to ask for her hand in marriage."

Ben felt as though he'd been hit by a truck. "I—" What could he say? That was exactly the conclusion Kate herself had wanted him to draw. Did Ben have the right to set him straight without Kate's permission?

What a mess. Somehow Ben had managed to get himself into a situation where he was working with Bianca to appear to woo Kate, while at the same time he was working with Kate to *fool* Bianca into thinking he was doing just that, and in both plans he was required to fool Henry Gregory into thinking the romance was real.

It was indeed a tangled web.

And Ben wasn't at all sure how to get out of it. Who would he hurt the most by telling the truth and cutting his losses? He wasn't all that worried about Bianca, but he didn't want to betray Kate.

"Speak up, young man," Henry prompted expectantly.

Ben cleared his throat, trying to buy whatever time he could, then said, "There's a good possibility that's in our future."

"The future? If your feelings are genuine, then why not now?"

"I'm not sure we're ready yet."

"Not ready or not serious about each other?" Henry demanded. "I heard you talking to Bianca about convincing me that you and Kate are together and now, though you say you care for her, you're not sure you have a future together. I'm not a fool, Devere, I know Bianca wanted to make me believe Kate was getting married so I would condone her own marriage. Your story just doesn't hold up."

"But Kate and I never said we were getting married."

"No." Henry tapped his chin. "No, you didn't. That's why I have been unsure about your intentions. I must confess, knowing your fine family has made me hope your feelings for my daughter were real." He hesitated. "But, given what I've heard tonight, I can only conclude one of two things. Either you're a liar and you're leading my one daughter on in return for a favor from my other daughter, or you and my Katherine are both lying to me."

The man had a good point and good reason to be upset. Ben didn't like being part of any of this.

So he decided to come clean.

"You're forgetting another possibility," Ben said, feeling his way through the words even as he was thinking them. Kate would probably kill him for giving the charade up, and Bianca would undoubtedly pout, but he wasn't going to lie anymore.

"What other possibility?"

"That Kate and I began this as a game to help Bianca, exactly as you suspected, but that—speaking only for myself now—the feelings became real."

That was exactly what happened. Even as he said it, Ben realized that that was exactly what had happened. And he was glad. Glad to feel it and glad to finally say it out loud.

"I'm in love with Kate," he concluded.

It wasn't often that Henry Gregory was taken by surprise, but he sure looked it now. "You're admitting it was a ruse but saying you've fallen in love with Katherine?"

Man, he really should be telling Kate this before telling her father. But, on the other hand, there were good reasons to be confiding in Henry Gregory. "That's exactly what I'm saying. I've fallen in love with your daughter. And I'd like your permission to have her hand in marriage."

They were interrupted by the sound of the door opening, then a woman's voice saying, "Oh, Henry, darling, there you are! My goodness, I have been trying to find a private place for us to slip away all night!" Footsteps came bustling across the floor, but Ben didn't need to see the woman to know who it was that was planning a romantic rendezvous with Kate's father.

It was his mother.

Chapter Twelve

It seemed as if it took forever for Kate to free herself from Erin Dalton's decorating tour of the house. The whole time she was gone, all she could think about was Ben and how great he looked and how nice it had been to walk into the party with him, and how she was starting to think about him a lot when he wasn't around.

At first she'd told herself it was just a testament to how boring the remaining bachelors of Avon Lake were, but she was beginning to realize it was really much more. Ben was funny and smart and everything she could want in a man. And then some.

In a way he'd been here all along—how could she have overlooked that for so many years?

She had to talk to him. She wasn't at all sure what she was going to say, but she had to find him. The need to do so was increasing by the moment.

When he finally emerged, it was from a hallway behind the foyer and she just happened to be standing there.

"Where have you been?" she asked, surprised at his sudden appearance.

"Just having a little talk with your dad," he said, and though the words were light, the expression on his face and the tone of his voice told her the conversation had been anything *but* light.

"What happened?" she asked, immediately on guard. "Has he figured out what we're doing?"

Ben gave a laugh. "Oh, yeah. Long since."

"Oh, no." Bianca was going to be so disappointed. But worse, she thought, what had her father done to Ben? "Was he very angry?" she asked, knowing, even as the words left her lips, that it was a stupid question. Of course he'd been angry!

"He was…" Ben hesitated. "Actually, he was quite insightful. He figured out exactly what we were doing and why. And he knew Bianca was behind the whole thing."

Kate gave an *of course* shrug, since Bianca was always behind every foolish and/or dangerous plan.

"But I don't think he's that upset," Ben concluded.

"What?" She had to have heard him wrong. If she knew her father—and she did—he would have blown a gasket upon getting confirmation that her children were all trying to dupe him. "That's not possible. He must have been furious."

"He looked like he might be heading that way for a minute or two, then—" Ben shrugged "—he wasn't. Actually, I think we reached an understanding."

"Oh, good Lord, what about?" She could only imagine what Ben might have said to try to impress her dad. Many guys had tried the same feat before, but it had never worked.

"About love, actually," he said. "About the fact that you never know when it's coming or where it's coming from."

She was completely confused now. "What are you talking about, Ben? You and my father talked about *love?*"

"Yes. We did."

"That's a little hard to imagine."

"Why? Because you can't imagine him being in love? Or you can't imagine me being in love?"

"Well, him—" She rolled her eyes. "That's obviously not going to happen anytime soon, but you…" She stopped and thought about what he was saying.

What *was* he saying?

"You talked to him about being in love?" she asked.

He nodded. "Yes."

"When were you last in love?" she asked cagily.

He smiled. "I've only been in love once in my life."

She dared not hope he was talking about her, yet she couldn't help but wonder why he was looking at her in that funny way and why his dimples were showing even though he wasn't actually smiling at her.

It was more as though he was trying *not* to smile.

"And you told my father about that," she said, eyeing him, trying to read his response.

He wasn't giving it up too easily. "Mmm-hmm."

"Why?"

Ben looked at her for a long moment and then reached out to take her arm. "Let's go for a little walk, okay, Kate? I think there's a pond out back. We can go skip rocks."

She went with him, but said, along the way, "I'm asking you why you're talking to my father about hearts and butterflies and you want to take me out to skip rocks on a pond?"

"Would you rather be in a stuffy room with all those stuffy people?" he asked, glancing back toward the house, which was practically alive with light out there in the dark night.

Suddenly the dark night was looking pretty inviting to Kate.

"Okay," she said when they got to the edge of the pond. "Spill it. What were you and my father talking about?"

"Bianca. You. My mother."

"Your *mother?*"

He gave a laugh and skimmed a stone all the way across the pond. "Wait till you hear about *that.*"

"Ben, you're making me nervous."

He skimmed another stone, then turned to her and put his hands on her arms. "I bet."

He was teasing her. She knew it. This was yet another way he had of being exasperating. Kate had the feeling she was going to be learning a lot about that. "Listen, mister, you tell me what's going on or I'll…I'll—"

"You'll what?"

She raised her chin. "Are you willing to take a chance on finding out?"

He laughed and pulled her close. "All right, all right, I'm sorry. It's not fair to yank your chain like this."

"Right. So tell me what happened."

"I told your father about our deal."

Whatever she was expecting him to say, it certainly wasn't that. Kate felt as if she'd been punched in the stomach. "You *told* him?"

Ben nodded. "I had to. He overheard me talking to Bianca. He knew something was up and I decided it was finally time to tell him the truth. The whole truth."

Kate swallowed. "What truth did you tell him?"

"That Bianca made a deal with me to pretend to date you. She said she was willing to give up the essence of Fireflight if I succeeded."

Kate stood ramrod-straight. "You made a deal with *Bianca?*"

"Relax." He touched her hair. "Right after I talked to her, I talked to you. I wasn't going to try to fool you into thinking something was happening when it wasn't."

"Good…"

"Thing is, there *was* something happening. I think from the moment I saw you again here, I began to fall for you." He stopped, reconsidering. "Maybe I'd already fallen for you, a long time ago, and this was just a reminder. I don't know."

Kate listened to him, barely able to breathe. He'd fallen for her? After all their sparring, and flirting, and fighting, did he really feel the same way about her that she did about him?

"So what did you tell my father?"

"That I love you. That I want to marry you. That I don't care about Bianca's deal or anything else, I would just do anything in my power to make you happy."

Her chest felt tight. Suddenly it was hard to breathe, but strangely enough she wasn't panicked, just…anticipating.

Something good was coming up.

"What are you saying, Ben?"

"I'm saying I love you, Kate. I think I've always loved you. And I *know* I always will."

"You…do?"

"Mmm-hmm."

Their eyes locked, then slowly Ben moved toward her. Kate stood still, hardly able to believe that what was happening was real. Suddenly her life felt like a scene from a movie that she never wanted to stop watching.

She hoped he'd kiss her—the hero kissing the heroine after a whole movie of bickering—and he didn't let her down.

His lips grazed lightly across hers and it was as light as a butterfly kiss. She didn't realize until a second afterward that she had leaned in and kissed him back and was now standing in front of him, in serious danger of toppling over right into him if he didn't take her into his arms again right away.

A moment rested in stillness between them.

Then Ben's mouth descended on hers again, but

this time it was hungrier, more insistent. This was no butterfly kiss, but a full-fledged, passionate kiss. His tongue touched hers and the touch sent a shock of electricity through her core.

There was no turning back, no saying no. She wrapped her arms around his neck and shoulders, and pulled him closer to her, hungrily exploring his mouth with her own, meeting him move for move.

The sound of their mingled breaths increased in the small space between them.

Ben ran a strong hand down to the small of Kate's back. His rough fingertips touched lightly on her lower back. A tingle of excitement arched Kate toward him and her hands rose to feel, once again, his soft, thick hair.

A pulse throbbed in her abdomen and increased in strength. It was want, it was need, and it was something else she couldn't quite identify.

Could it really be love?

Now *that* was something she wasn't prepared to admit. She drew back, breathless.

"We can't do this," she gasped.

"Yes, we can." He reached for her.

She pushed his hand down with a little less force than she would have liked. "No, we can't. Seriously, Ben, it would be a mistake. We don't want to get embroiled."

"We're already embroiled." He put his hand on her shoulder and trailed it down her arm. "More embroiled than we'd planned to be."

"But we can't be. I live here and you live in Dallas, and even though I want to move there eventually, I'm not there now and you're going back and…" She swallowed, then continued. "It just could never work."

"It could totally work. Kate, I l—"

"Don't say it." She raised a hand. "Don't say it. There's no way you can finish that sentence without taking it all the way and I'm not sure you're ready to do that."

Ben gave a laugh. "Stop trying to micromanage me, Kate. I know what I'm doing. And I know I love you. And I know I want to marry you."

Warmth washed over her face. "You want to…" She swallowed again, hard. "You want to what?"

"You heard me." He got down on his knee in front of her and took her hands in his. "We've been through it all, Kate, throughout our whole lives. But you've never really left my mind and I've got to think there's a reason for that."

She took a short breath. "Other than obsessive-compulsive disorder, you mean?"

He laughed. "They've got medicine for that. Unfortunately there's no antidote for what I've got. Except, of course, for you. All day, every day. For the rest of my life." He took her hand and put it to his lips, with the lightest kiss. "So what do you say, Kate? Think you could take a chance on me? I promise I won't let you down."

She was so filled with emotion that she could barely breathe. "Aren't you worried about me letting you down?" she asked. "I'm the one who hasn't been willing to hold on to a boyfriend around here."

He laughed outright. "Of course not! You were waiting for me."

She smiled. "Ah-hh…is that right? And I didn't even know it."

"Nah, you didn't know it, but that's what you were doing." He kissed her again and she responded in kind. Then he pulled back. "So, what's your answer, Miss Gregory? You willing to take a chance on a guy like me, who sets fireworks off practically right in your hand?"

"Oh, you've been setting fireworks off, all right," she said, lifting her hand to cup his cheek. "I guess that was always a harbinger of things to come."

"Meaning it's fate," he supplied. "And your answer is…?"

"My answer is yes," she said, and was surprised by a sudden onslaught of tears. "Yes. I will marry you."

Ben gave a huge whoop of glee as he stood up and grabbed her, pulling her into his arms. "It may be a gamble, but it's the best bet you'll ever make."

"It's the only bet I'll make. The *last* bet of my life. From now on, I want to deal in certainties, not gambles."

"But this time…?"

"For you, I'll take the chance."

"Shrewd Lady to win." He chuckled and touched her mouth. "These are the highest stakes you'll ever take."

"Good." She smiled. "Because they're going to have to last forever. And this time, I have a feeling they will."

Epilogue

Avon Lake Country Club had never looked so festive. There were white roses on every table, tiny glowing gold stars hanging from the ceiling, candles everywhere, creating a radiance of light. The air was alive with excitement and happiness.

The table by the French doors to the terrace held one of the biggest wedding cakes anyone in the town had ever seen; vanilla cake with coconut cream frosting—the bride's favorite.

"It was a beautiful wedding," Lynn Finnegan said to Kate, dabbing her eyes with a handkerchief then giving her a hug. "So romantic." She walked away, sniffling and repeating, "So wonderfully romantic."

Kate turned to Ben and smiled. "It *was* romantic, wasn't it? Releasing the doves was such a perfect symbol of our families putting away their past competitiveness."

"It was a great idea." He put his arm around her and squeezed gently. He smelled of fresh soap, with just the faintest woodsy undertone. Already it was a scent that she associated with comfort and safety. "Imagine, Gregory Farms and the Devere Ranch will be Gregory-Devere Farms. Who would have believed it?"

"No one," she agreed.

"After everything I did, thinking I was just trying to get Fireflight to sire one of our mares, and we end up with all of this. A complete merger. Literally."

Kate raised an eyebrow. "I think it will benefit all involved."

"So they'll survive without us when we go to Dallas, you think?"

She looked dubious. "It's only an hour's drive."

Bianca and Victor came up to them, hand-in-hand.

"Wasn't it beautiful?" Bianca bubbled. "I hope my wedding will be at least half as romantic!"

"With you taking a year and a half to plan the thing, I'm pretty sure yours will be *twice* as romantic. And six times as expensive." Kate laughed. "You'll make sure of it."

"You bet I will."

"Now, Bianca, you know Kate," Victor said, patting Bianca's arm. "She never bets. She's way too sensible for that."

Kate and Ben exchanged a glance.

"I'm only getting married once," Bianca said. "And I worked hard for it."

"*You* worked hard for it?" Kate repeated. "Honey, we *all* worked hard for it. Don't take all the credit for yourself, you had a veritable army working for your wedding."

"You're right," Bianca said sincerely. "It's thanks to you and Ben most of all."

"Ladies and gentlemen, if I could have your attention." The orchestra leader tapped on his microphone. "The bride and groom are going to have their first dance as husband and wife." He turned to the band and signaled them to begin playing "Moonlight Serenade."

Kate's eyes filled with tears and she felt Ben take her hand and lead her toward the dance floor.

They stopped at the edge and watched as their parents—her father and his mother—stepped out to take their first dance as Mr. and Mrs. Henry Gregory.

"I can't believe it," Kate whispered to Ben. "I still can't believe my eyes. They fell in love so quickly."

"It must run in our families," he said, then took her by the elbow and led her out onto the terrace. "Come with me."

They opened the door and walked out into the unusually balmy night. The stars dotted the sky like diamonds on blue velvet.

"Are we alone?" Ben asked.

Kate looked around, then laughed. "I think we are. Why? Are you going to take advantage of me?"

"Every chance I get. But there's more important business to take care of first."

"I thought we did that!"

"Exactly what I'm talking about. Here." He reached into his pocket and produced two gleaming gold wedding rings. "I hate that we haven't been wearing these."

"Me, too."

"I just want to go in there and make an announcement to everyone in town. Now, give me your hand."

Kate giggled like a schoolgirl with a secret as she held out her left hand for him to slip her wedding band on her finger.

He had done it for the first time just twenty-four hours before, in a surprisingly quaint and simple wedding chapel in Las Vegas. It had been raining outside and Ben had put his jacket over Kate's head as they'd run inside, laughing all the way.

* * *

"Is rain a good omen or a bad omen?" Kate teased.

"Honey, right now everything's a good omen." Ben gave the smile that took her breath away every time. *"We've got nothing but good coming our way now."*

"So the rain is just…washing away our sins, or whatever the saying is."

Now came the pirate smile. *"Until tonight."*

Her heart tripped at the thought.

He opened the carved wooden door and stood in the rain, letting her go in first. When she turned to face him in the lobby of the building, his dark hair was damp with the rain but his blue eyes shone like the sun. He had never looked more handsome.

It occurred to Kate that for the rest of her life, every time it rained she would think of this moment and smile.

"Mr. Devere and Ms. Gregory?" an older woman asked from behind Kate.

Kate turned to see a woman who might have been the grandmother in any old-fashioned kid's movie. She had soft gray hair, loosely piled in a bun, and gentle eyes.

"That's us," Kate said to her.

"I've already prepared your marriage license

and I have it right here. If you're ready, my husband is ready to perform the ceremony."

Kate's chest tightened and she turned to Ben. "Are we ready?"

He put his hands on her shoulders. "Katherine Gregory, this is the happiest moment of my life. I'm more than ready, I've been waiting for this forever." The way he looked at her, with such intensity of feeling, made her feel weak in the knees.

Ben looked at her that way again now.

"Mrs. Devere." He lifted her hand to his lips, looked into her eyes and said, "I love you."

She melted a little bit inside. "I love you, too." Her eyes filled with tears. "You'd better hold me up because my knees are going weak."

"It's my intention to make sure you feel like that every day of your life."

She'd never felt so happy, so completely fulfilled in her life. But also, she'd never felt so completely at peace. Her father and his mother had fallen in love and now Ben's family farm was saved by virtue of joining forces with her family's. Better still, neither of their parents would suffer the loneliness they'd endured so much recently.

As for herself and Ben…well, she knew that being with Ben was the right decision. What scared

her was how close she had come to never knowing it.

It didn't bear thinking about.

"Come on," she said to him, "give me yours."

He handed her his wedding band and she put it
on his finger, saying, "You and me, forever and ever."

"And ever." He pulled her into his arms and held
her tight, kissing the top of her head. "I can't wait to
tell everyone about our little trip to Vegas yesterday."

"I know, but today is their day." She put her arms
around his back and closed her eyes, remembering the
blur of colorful neon, the white chapel, the red carpet
on the aisle. She could recall the smells, the sounds,
everything, in bright vivid color. It had been quirky and
tacky, and she'd loved it. "We have the rest of our lives
to celebrate our marriage. In fact, I think we should
go back to Vegas every year and renew our vows."

"How about every week?"

"I could do that, too!"

"I might just hold you to that." He pulled her
close and said, lowly, "Care to dance, Mrs. Devere?"

"Absolutely, Mr. Devere."

The music of the orchestra inside was faint but
clear. It felt, to Kate, as if the wind was carrying the
song just for them.

"Now *this* is romantic," Ben said as they swayed
slowly, like leaves in the breeze.

"You know, this is where we were when I first started to fall in love with you."

"Yeah?" His eyes were bright with surprise. "Tell me."

"When you gave me your jacket and we had that horrible beer." She crinkled her nose at the memory. "That's when I started to…I don't know, to see you. Of course, I didn't realize it at the time."

"Good thing I came to that function, then. I almost didn't." He raised his eyebrows. "And the beer wasn't bad."

"I'm more of a champagne girl myself." She raised an eyebrow. "That's something you should know about me now."

"I already know that about you. You are champagne to my beer, and diamonds to my steel, and silk to my burlap. You make everything in my life just a little more beautiful and soft and…bubbly."

She laughed. "Bubbly was a bit of a stretch."

"I know." He laughed. "I'm not a poet. But you get the point. You've made everything in my life better, and I can't wait to see what the future holds for us."

"Me, too."

They stopped dancing and he smiled down on her. "Hey. There's just one thing I need now."

"What's that?"

He touched her cheek. "Kiss me, Kate."
And she did.
Again and again.

* * * * *

*There's one more romance in store for these
women of Avon, Texas. Be sure to watch for
TWELFTH NIGHT PROPOSAL, coming only to
Silhouette Romance in December 2005.*

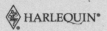

HARLEQUIN®
Presents
Seduction and Passion Guaranteed!

Don't miss our two Christmas-themed stories,
coming in December 2005 only from
Harlequin Presents®!

THE GREEK'S CHRISTMAS BABY
Lucy Monroe
#2506

Greek tycoon Aristide Kouros has a piece of paper to prove
that he's married, but no memory of his beautiful wife, Eden.
Eden loves Aristide, and it's breaking her heart that he has no
recollection of their love. But Eden has a secret that
will bind Aristide to her forever....

CLAIMING HIS
CHRISTMAS BRIDE
Carole Mortimer
#2510

When Gideon Webber meets Molly Barton he wants her badly.
But he is convinced she is another man's mistress.... Three
years on, a chance meeting throws Molly back in his path, and
this time he's determined to claim Molly—as his wife!

SILHOUETTE Romance®

COMING NEXT MONTH

#1794 TWELFTH NIGHT PROPOSAL—Karen Rose Smith
Shakespeare in Love
Sometimes tragedy highlights the greatness of love. Of course, Verity
Sumpter, who lost her twin, and Leo Montgomery, who lost his wife,
wouldn't believe it at first. Yet, as they draw closer, they just might
see that the barriers of mistrust that loss erects are best scaled in
pairs.

#1795 THE DATING GAME—Shirley Jump
Matilda Grant prefers the Survival TV show she'd applied for
originally. At least *there* the chameleons sometimes reveal
themselves. On this dating game, she can't tell if she should trust
her heart, the bachelors, or—no, probably not—that charmingly
ubiquitous David Simpson....

#1796 MEET ME UNDER THE MISTLETOE—
Julianna Morris
Sure, the breezy Shannon O'Rourke coaxed his son's cherished toy
rabbit from his grasp—a rare sign of outreach from a child who had
just lost his mother. Still, Alex McKenzie is unsettled by her vibrant
presence...and the hope she plants in his lonely heart.

#1797 BOUND BY HONOR—Donna Clayton
Men of Honor
Gage Dalton owes Jenna Butler a Life Gift because she saved him
during a storm. Yet, even as she makes him marry her, so to better lobby
the Tribe for guardianship of her niece, he wonders if perhaps he isn't
receiving the more wonderful gift himself....

SRCNMNOV05